PRAISE FOR *DEAR SWEET PEA*

Kirkus Reviews Best Children's Book
IndieBound Indie Next List Top Ten Pick
Texas Lone Star Reading List Selection
Reading the West Book Awards, Young Readers Winner
YALSA Best Fiction for Young Adults Nominee
Cybils Awards Nominee, Middle Grade Fiction
Goodreads Choice Award Nominee, Middle Grade
Amazon Editors' Best Book of the Year (Ages 9–12)

★ "Murphy creates a wonderfully realistic portrait
of tween life in her first middle grade novel.
Sweet Pea is a treasure of a protagonist."
—ALA *Booklist* (starred review)

★ "Endearing and funny. An excellent blend of
eccentricity, humor, genuine sweetness, and mild drama."
—*Kirkus Reviews* (starred review)

★ "With gentle humor, ageless wisdom, and charming,
genuine characters who represent a diversity
of experiences, Murphy's novel offers all the emotional
highs and lows of pitch-perfect middle grade."
—*Publishers Weekly* (starred review)

Dear Sweet Pea

JULIE MURPHY

BALZER + BRAY

An Imprint of HarperCollinsPublishers

Balzer + Bray is an imprint of HarperCollins Publishers.

Dear Sweet Pea
Copyright © 2019 by Julie Murphy
Illustrations © 2019 by Michelle Cunningham and
Ambient Ideas / Shutterstock (stack of paper with clip)
All rights reserved. Printed in the United States of America.
No part of this book may be used or reproduced in any manner whatsoever
without written permission except in the case of brief quotations embodied in
critical articles and reviews. For information address HarperCollins Chil-
dren's Books, a division of HarperCollins Publishers, 195 Broadway,
New York, NY 10007.
www.harpercollinschildrens.com

ISBN 978-0-06-247308-0

Typography by Jenna Stempel-Lobell
20 21 22 23 24   PC/BRR 10 9 8 7 6 5 4 3 2 1
❖
First paperback edition, 2021

For Vivienne and Aurelia, my sweet peas

Sometimes, what you're looking for is already there.
—Aretha Franklin

CHAPTER ONE

The Cat's Out of the Box

I've counted my birthday savings three times, and at this rate, I don't think I'll ever have enough money to clone myself. I guess it doesn't help that cloning people isn't really a thing yet. Trust me, if it was, my mom would've already taken me in to make an identical model. One for her. One for Dad. Easy-peasy lemon squeezy.

But since there can only be one Sweet Pea, my parents have decided that the next best way to deal with their divorce is to have two houses. Two completely separate houses on the same street that look just about as identical as two different houses could. Similar paint and rugs and even furniture. Mom gets the original, and Dad gets the dupe, which makes sense since the old house belonged to Nana—Mom's mom—before she died.

I've spent a lot of time thinking about which of my things to take to Dad's house, but I'm what Mrs. Young calls a "visual learner," so this morning Oscar Rivera, my best (and only) friend, and I took an old roll of Dad's blue painter's tape and split my room in two. It reminds me of the blue line down the middle of the gym that Coach Jeffers uses for dodgeball, which, if you ask me, is even crueler than the section on rope climbing we did last fall. Not only do your classmates have a popularity death match picking teams, but then they get to peg you with rubber balls too. Hopefully packing up my room won't be quite as traumatic.

"What's your mom gonna say when she comes home and finds your room like this?" Oscar asks, his shiny black hair swirled into a perfect mold, using his latest discovery from the drugstore: pomade, a sticky hair product that comes in a glass jar and Oscar swears is a miracle.

I shrug as I take a second to process the damage. My room looks like someone came in with a giant eraser and just wiped away half of the whole place, leaving the other side in its usual state of perfectly organized mess—unmade bed, mismatching socks stuffed under the bed, and stacks of old homework and newspaper clippings piled up on my nightstand. "I won't be home to find out. It's Dad's night."

Since there are only seven days in a week, every other week Mom and Dad take turns with who gets me for three nights and who gets four nights. Mom says it's "imperative" that neither of them is perceived as the "dominant parent," but if you ask me, all you have to do to figure out which of my parents is in charge is ask yourself who's making the rules to begin with. If you guessed Mom—*ding, ding, ding!*—you're right.

I split the books by alphabetical order. Mom's house gets *A* through *M* and Dad's house gets the rest. The division of all my other belongings was much slower and more snooze-worthy. But as Oscar constantly reminds me, if I ever need anything, I'll be two houses down the street, separated only by Miss Flora Mae's hulking two-story house.

"At least you didn't cut your sheets in half," he says and reaches down for a box with *SWEET PEA'S DESK STUFF* scrawled across the side.

"Lift with your knees!" I say, mimicking what I've heard Mr. McMullan shout at his employees from behind his desk at Love's Hardware.

"I wasn't built for grunt work," says Oscar as he heads for the door. "You got the last box?"

"Yup. See you over there."

I squat down to tape the flaps of the final box shut before standing, doing my best to lift with my knees. What does that even mean anyway? And why did I cram so much stuff in this box?

But then, just as I steady myself, a growling meow vibrates from inside the box.

"Holy crud!" I snap and drop it on the rug. Another meow, this one a little softer. "Oh, Cheese! I'm so sorry." I rip the tape from the box. "Cheese, you gotta forgive me, buddy."

Cheese is my fifteen-pound orange tabby. No wonder the thing was heavier than I expected! He leaps from the box full of random desk clutter and saunters out of my bedroom, his tail slapping the door frame.

"Cheese!" I call once more. "I wasn't paying attention. I'm sorry." What can I say? The cat can hold a grudge. Like kitty, like owner.

I tap my index finger to the side of my head, hoping I'll remember to give him a few extra treats tonight to make up for my rude behavior. Cheese was our big family Christmas present when I was six years old. I was given the honor of choosing his name and decided to call him Cheese, because he . . . looked like cheese? I don't know. I was six, okay? In hindsight, I should have named him after my favorite cheese: Havarti.

With a sigh, I give up on the tape and fold the flaps of the box over before taking one last glimpse at my room. Crisp white trim with peach wallpaper and newspaper and magazine clippings pinned randomly all over every surface. A few *Miss Flora Mae I?* advice column classics, neat pictures of places I can't even believe exist from Dad's *National Geographic* subscription, and a few strips from the comics section of the *Valentine Gazette*. I still remember painting the trim with Mom and Dad and the way Mom squealed when Dad ran a wet paintbrush down her back.

I think I sort of get what adults mean when they say, "If these walls could talk." Let's be real, though. The thought of talking walls spooks me out big-time.

As I step backward out the front door of the house, the screen door creaks as it shuts behind me. "Goodbye, home," I whisper mournfully.

"A tad dramatic, don't you think?" calls Oscar.

I whirl around.

"Just wanted to make sure you didn't need any more help." He stands on the sidewalk. "Didn't mean to interrupt your big moment."

I huff, blowing my thick black bangs into the air. "I wasn't having a moment." I look back at the house—a red-brick one-story with white trim and a bright-blue door (Mom's addition)—only slightly different from every other house on the block except Miss Flora Mae's. "Okay, maybe I was."

"And the Academy Award goes to . . . Sweet Pea DiMarco!"

I look off into the distance. "I'd like to thank the little people—and by little people, I mean my best friend, Oscar. My Academy Award is the most exciting thing to ever happen to him, so let's have a moment of silence for how sad that is."

"Har, har," he says. "You know I'm the talent in this relationship."

I laugh. "If you're the talent, I'm the brains."

He swings the gate open for me. "Well, let's get a move on it. I'm starved. And I was promised pizza in exchange for physical labor."

"Don't pretend like you wouldn't have done it for free," I say, walking through the gate. "You love me. I'm your best friend."

He laughs dryly. "You're my only real friend." He points to Cheese sitting in the window. "Did you hear that, Cheese? I'm her *best* friend!"

That gets a real laugh out of me. One time when Oscar was spending the night, Cheese fell asleep on his face. Oscar woke up sneezing every five seconds. I explained to him that it was a sign of affection, but Oscar, who is just a little bit allergic to just about everything, swore that Cheese had a jealous vendetta against him.

Outside of Cheese, though, Oscar *is* my best friend and I'm his, but since my parents announced their divorce—or as my mom called it, their "mindful division"—he's been there every step of the way, and somehow it's brought us even closer.

We walk in silence past Miss Flora Mae's house, where we can see her sitting in her sunroom on her typewriter, watching us over the top of her gold reading glasses. Her long silver hair is wrapped into a bun on the top of her head, and her white skin is soft with wrinkles that I used to always want to trace with my finger when I was little.

Miss Flora Mae's house is the only two-story house on the block. A long time ago it was a pure white with black shutters, but now it's a little dingy, with graying edges and chipping paint. The big wraparound porch and the second-floor balcony are still a pretty incredible sight. But I guess people figured out that scientists weren't lying when they say heat rises, because out here in Valentine, Texas, where it looks like someone just plopped our town down in the middle of a desert, no one really messes around with tall buildings unless they have to. So Miss Flora Mae owns one of the few two-story houses on this side of town, which was mostly built up in the last fifty or sixty years.

Oscar looks away quickly, careful not to make eye contact with my neighbor.

"She's not gonna put a curse on you," I tell him.

He shakes his head. "That lady knows everyone's dirt. She's like your mom, except your mom actually has to *keep* everyone's secrets. It's her job. But people just write Miss

Flora Mae and dump out all their feelings for her advice column. She's bound to know something awful about everyone in this town."

He's right. Mom's obligated to keep secrets in a way Miss Flora Mae isn't. Mom calls it "doctor-patient confidentiality." Heck, even when someone says hi to her at the grocery store and I try to nose around to find out if they're even a client of hers, she winks and says something about everyone knowing everyone in this town.

"Well, you've never written to Miss Flora Mae," I tell him, "so you've got nothing to worry about—unless there's something you're not telling me . . ."

He rolls his eyes. "Trust me. I'm not that desperate."

His reaction makes me clam up. I've written Miss Flora Mae three times in my life, and not once has she ever written back. It's the kind of thing I try to push to the furthest corner of my brain along with every other unanswered question I have.

Dutifully, Oscar opens the gate to the house just on the other side of Miss Flora Mae's, and I trudge up the steps to my dad standing in the doorway.

This house was only empty for two weeks after the Cordova family moved out before Mom came up with her "genius" idea for Dad to live on the same street as us. For the last four months, Dad lived in the El Cosmico Hotel in a room with two double beds so that I could come over and stay with him. During the day the El Cosmico is a pretty run-down place, but at night, when it was harder to see the dust and dead roly-polies in the windowsill, I actually sort of liked sitting out by the pool with Dad under the glow of the flashing hot-pink letters and neon-green cactus of the sign. But I know Dad was getting pretty down with motel life and not having a real kitchen to cook in.

"It's a big night," Dad says. "First night in the new house." He throws his arms up, gesturing to the house behind him. "Not too shabby, huh, Sweet Pea? And I've got some curry chicken pot pie in the oven." Dad pushes his fingers through his hair. Mom used to call it one of his nervous tics—fidgeting with his hair. I'm white, like both my parents, but like Dad I've got an olive-y undertone and have the same black hair as he does. It's wiry and thick, like his bushy eyebrows, which it looks like he passed on to me too.

I give the tiny porch one good look, trying my best to give this place a chance. The only thing that makes this house feel more like home than Mom's place is Dad's beat-up work truck out front—a black pickup with a bed full of scaffolding and painting supplies. "Same street. New house."

"I even painted the door to match," he points out. And sure as heck, he did. "I was thinking we'd get a porch swing just like—"

"Mom's," I say flatly. I shake my head and point to the door. "You got the wrong shade of blue." I feel immediately bad as I turn to Oscar and say, "Let's go."

Sometimes Oscar says the wrong things at the wrong times, but right now he's got my back and follows me into my room in my new second home. And because he's a true best friend, he even slams my bedroom door for me because my hands are full.

CHAPTER TWO

The Most Important Meal of the Day

"Sweet Pea?" asks my dad as he knocks on my bedroom door the next morning. "First breakfast in the new house! How do you want your bacon?"

"You can come in," I tell him, the covers pulled up over my face. In the last year, Dad has gotten a little weird around me. He's careful about giving me plenty of time to answer him before he comes into my bedroom, and the last time I had to dress up for Easter Sunday, he said my dress was flattering. Flattering! What kind of word is that?

It started two years ago when he was pulling the laundry out of the dryer and held up my training bra for both me and my mom to see. He laughed and told my mom he must have accidentally shrunken one of her sports bras.

11

The laughter stopped immediately when he noticed the color draining from my face. I yanked it out of his hands and marched to my room, slamming the door behind me. (I guess you could say I've got a thing for slamming doors.) It wasn't his fault. He didn't know. But the whole suddenly-having-to-wear-a-bra thing is bad enough without making it Dad's business too.

I moan from beneath the covers. Spending the night without Cheese felt just plain wrong. After Oscar and I shared a pizza with Dad, I tried bringing Cheese over here to stay with me, but he kept pawing at the screen door. Mom even bought him an identical litter box for Dad's house and went through the effort of sifting out clumps from his old litter box to mix in with his new litter so he'd recognize his scent. That's real dedication. But it's like Cheese is staging his own one-cat revolution and he's the only one who's not playing along with this "mirror living" nonsense.

"Extra crispy on the bacon," I tell my dad. "And scrambled cheesy on the eggs."

"Cheesy eggs and super-dead bacon. Coming right up!"

I wait for the door to close behind him before I throw my sheets back and slink out of bed.

Last night was my first solo night with Dad at his new house, and this morning will be our first solo breakfast. I guess most families get together for dinner, but with Mom's crazy client schedule, our thing was always breakfast. So rolling out of this bed knowing that only Dad will be waiting at the kitchen table makes Monday morning feel even more *Monday* than it already does.

I reach into my closet and pull out my own personal uniform—jean shorts, black high-top sneakers, and a black-and-white-striped T-shirt. Dad wears the same coveralls to work every day. When I was a kid I asked him why he never wore different colors, and he said that geniuses wear the same thing every day so they can save their brain power for more important decisions. I don't know if I'm a genius, but I like the idea of saving brain power. So for me, it's usually dark shorts, pants, or even a skirt and a black-and-white-striped shirt. Sometimes a headband if I'm feeling sassy. Miss Flora Mae says I always look like I've just robbed a bank, but that she can appreciate my consistency—whatever that means. My closet might be a little boring, but at least it makes it a smidge easier to deal with the limited clothing options out there for a thirteen-year-old girl who's nearly sized out of the juniors' department.

After getting dressed in a striped T-shirt, black denim shorts, and a yellow headband, I shut the door to my new bedroom behind me and stand there for a minute in the dark hallway. Dad's bedroom, with the door wide open, sits at the end of the hallway, but just past my room is something Mom's house never had—a third bedroom. I think Dad's third bedroom probably just has a bunch of his old stuff in it. But I feel a little funny going in it since the door is closed.

Most houses on our street have only two bedrooms. They're all the same style—except, of course, Miss Flora Mae's, which has a style all its own. I call Mom's house Sweet Pea Headquarters 1.0. We used to live in an apartment above Mom's practice downtown, but when Nana died when I was in kindergarten, she left us her house, and it's been home ever since. Dad's house—or Sweet Pea Headquarters 2.0—is the bigger version, with a third bedroom and a wider garage.

Dad tried buying furniture that looks like all the stuff in SPHQ 1.0, but there's no good way to copy Nana's kitchen table, complete with scratches on the legs from when Cheese was a kitten. The whole place kind of reminds me of the Halloween costume I bought at Green's Grocers last year. From far away, I looked exactly like the zombie prom queen I'd envisioned in my head, but the longer I looked, the easier it was to see that nothing about my costume was close enough to the real deal to actually be scary. Honestly, the scariest part about it was the tag on the inside that said *KEEP AWAY FROM OPEN FLAME! HIGHLY FLAMMABLE MATERIAL!*

In the kitchen Dad is half-dressed in his usual gray coveralls with the top hanging around his waist and with a fresh undershirt up top. Mom never let him wear his coveralls in the house before, but now I guess Dad can make his own rules.

My dad is a painter. Not some fancy-schmancy art-school painter. He paints houses and buildings and rooms and basically anything that could need painting. Sometimes, though, businesses ask him to come paint designs in their windows, like for holidays or big sales. He's never said so, but part of me has always wondered if he secretly likes those special jobs best.

"How's the bacon?" Dad asks through a mouthful of hash browns.

I brush my toes against the leg of the kitchen table, just to be sure there are no claw scratches from Cheese. "Very dead," I tell him.

He kisses his fingers like a chef. "Maybe we could make some baked ziti tonight?" he asks. "Then catch up on *Jeopardy!*?"

"I think Mom has Mondays," I remind him. I moved in on a Sunday, and the plan is that Dad gets Friday, Saturday, and Sunday while Mom gets Monday, Tuesday, Wednesday, and each of them takes every other Thursday. If that sounds confusing to you, join the club. When Dad was still at the El Cosmico, we didn't have much of a schedule, but I guess him moving into an actual house made things feel more real.

He nods. "Right, right."

The thought of my dad, sitting here just two houses over eating dinner and watching *Jeopardy!* by himself while Mom and I are together is the kind of thing that stings. It reminds me that, despite my two matching bedrooms and the short walk between my parents' houses, they are divorced. D-I-V-O-R-C-E-D. No matter how pretty or normal they try to make it feel.

I still can't help but think they could have stuck it out. There had to be a better way.

Dad shakes out the paper and clears his throat. "'Dear Miss Flora Mae, my son is getting married to a big-city girl who's a little full of herself. She's a lawyer in Dallas and has got it in her head that no one will come out to her wedding if she has it out here in Valentine. How do I convince them that the West Texas landscape is the perfect backdrop for their dream wedding instead of that godforsaken concrete jungle known as Dallas? Yours truly, Mom on a Mission.'"

I squint, wiggling in my chair as I concentrate. Of all our family traditions, this is one of my favorites. Dad would read us Miss Flora Mae's advice column over breakfast while me and Mom took turns answering the letter aloud. Sometimes our answers were spot-on with Miss Flora Mae's, and other times, we were just as stumped as the person who'd written in. Mom's advice was always a little too perfect. The kind of stuff that sounds easy but is hard to actually do. My style was a little more down-to-earth. Nobody's perfect. What's the use in pretending?

"Sounds like this girl's a little bit of a bridezilla," says Dad.

"A what?" I can't help but picture a half lizard, half human in a puffy white wedding gown and glittering veil, slithering down the aisle, claws full of a bouquet of flowers and a tail dragging behind her.

Dad chuckles. "A monster bride," he says. "Someone who's hard to work with. Not all that flexible."

"Well, mayyyyyyybe this mom should just let her son's fiancée plan the wedding she wants?"

"Dear Mom on a Mission," Dad says in an official-sounding voice, "perhaps a parent's most noble mission is to do whatever will make their child happiest, and in this case that includes your future daughter-in-law's plans for her concrete-jungle wedding. This is one safari you won't want to miss."

"Clever," I say through a bite of cheesy eggs.

I finish my breakfast and fill up my water bottle before grabbing my backpack and lunch. I give Dad a quick hug goodbye and sprint to the bus stop at the end of the street before it leaves me behind. On the bus Oscar is waiting for me with a saved seat in the second row.

He lets out a yawn so big I can see his tonsils. "How was night one?"

I pause and think about telling him that I felt my whole body hiccup every time the house creaked in the middle of the night or that it was weird to see Dad's family pictures piled up in a box instead of hanging on the wall or that I couldn't find the hand soap when I went to the bathroom.

Instead, I shrug. "It was fine." I shake my head. Oh heck, who am I kidding? "It was weird," I blurt. "It was like waking up from a dream but then just finding out you're still dreaming. Like, it was my room, but it wasn't. Everything was just a little bit off."

"I don't know why your parents don't just do like what my tía and tío did. Tía Lisa kept the house and Tío Rudy got a tiny little one-room apartment at the edge of town before moving to Odessa after he met his new girlfriend in the Classifieds section of the newspaper."

Oscar comes from a large Mexican family and sometimes just listening to his mom talk on the phone to her sisters is more interesting than most TV shows, but his tía Lisa and tío Rudy were the first divorce in the family ever, making them the big family gossip for a long time now. "Aren't the Classifieds for, like, used furniture and odd jobs?"

His whole body flops dramatically when he shrugs. "Maybe people try to trade their boyfriends for recliners?"

"A recliner sounds way better than a boyfriend," I say, trying my best to hide the way the thought alone of a boyfriend makes my mouth go dry. "Well, I don't want my dad to move-move. You don't think he'd actually *do* that, do you? But maybe he doesn't have to live one house down from my mom, and maybe his place could look totally different. Like it's just his instead of *theirs*."

He shakes his head. "White people are weird."

CHAPTER THREE

The Comeback Kid Minus the Comebacks

Rochelle Cordova moved away four weeks ago, and nothing has been the same since. Rochelle was nice, I guess. We weren't exactly what I would call friends. But she changed my life in two major ways just by existing. First, her family moved out of the house that Dad is now renting, making this whole twinning-parent-freak-show thing possible.

Second, and more importantly, Rochelle was the ice cream in mine and Kiera Bryant's ice-cream sandwich, which is to say that in class she sat behind Kiera and in front of me. God bless anyone whose last name starts with the letter C, because unless Kiera or I drop dead or we get a new student with a C last name before the end of the school year in just a few weeks, Kiera and I are stuck sitting close enough to touch until the final bell of seventh grade rings.

Kiera. My ex-best friend. It'd be better if there was one simple reason why we stopped being friends, but it was the kind of thing that happened slowly and then all at once. She started hanging out with a group of girls in the next grade—the kind of girls who even make teachers feel uncool. She'd invite me to tag along with her, but it didn't take long before both of us figured out that I was way out of my league with her new friends. The more time we spent apart, the more reasons I found to be annoyed by her. But then we'd do something—with just the two of us—like slumber parties at my house or trips to the bowling alley while our dads played for their league, and I'd remember all over again why we were friends. Kiera was actually really funny as long as I wasn't the butt of the joke. But then the summer after fourth grade created too much space between us, and when we went back to school in August, it was a little too easy for hurt feelings to turn into a distance we couldn't seem to close up again. Mom says good things are worth fighting for, but sometimes it's hard to remember why something was good to begin with.

It was like I used to love chicken and dumplings until one day I had it and the chicken wasn't cooked all the way. I nearly ralphed right there in the middle of Honey's Diner. I was so grossed out that I haven't been able to bring myself to try it again, no matter how good it smells. Blech. Dad says it left a bad taste in my mouth.

So I wasn't too pleased when, after the weekend Rochelle and her family moved back to San Antonio, I came back to find Mrs. Young had ambushed us by removing Rochelle's desk and leaving me to stare at the back of Kiera Bryant's head, her braids gathered into a loose ponytail at the back of her neck. And now even though I can't see her face, I just know she's judging me. I can see it in the way her shoulder blades pinch together every time I open my mouth. Nobody new ever moves to Valentine, so the likelihood of our alphabetical dilemma carrying over into eighth grade is high.

I'm not a quiet or shy person. I'm not exactly loud either—okay, maybe a *touch* dramatic like Oscar says—but something about Kiera makes me quieter than a mouse. Like, I don't even want to breathe in the wrong direction in case she notices me and decides to remind me that, to her, I'm nothing more than her ex-BFF reject.

"Okay, class, I'm passing out the review for the life science test," says Mrs. Young, who's wearing bright-yellow pants and a navy-blue shirt with constellations stitched all over it.

I like Mrs. Young. For a teacher, she's pretty awesome. She's kind of round in a way that reminds me of myself if I were actually cool and knew what to do with my hair.

She also wears neat-colored lipstick like lavender or blue or orange.

"Don't forget to check out the bulletin board during morning break. There are some tips and tricks for your research projects."

I let out a loud groan. Ugh . . . the research project. I still haven't figured out who I'm going to pick for my project.

She clears her throat and continues. "And I've even added a few things relevant to your summer vacation, including information about the Valentine Community Theater's summer camp."

"Will Tabitha be there?" asks Samantha from the front row.

Mrs. Young's wife, Tabitha, is a firefighter and volunteers at the Valentine Community Theater teaching improvisation classes. They have a lizard named Persephone and a gray cat named Edith. I've only met Tabitha once, but I make a habit of trusting fellow cat owners.

Mrs. Young smiles at Samantha. "As much as her schedule will allow her!" And with that she sweeps her long dark-brown ringlets half up with a clip the same way she does every morning when it's time to get started on class work. "Take one and pass it back. And listen up very carefully: I'm not saying this is exactly what the test will look like, but I am saying that the review and the quiz could be fraternal twins." She winks dramatically so that no one can miss it.

Dusty Sanders, a short white boy with one uneven front tooth and short red spiky hair, shoots one hand up on the other side of the class, and he doesn't even wait to be called on. "What does fraternal twins even mean, miss? Is that like a college fraternity but only for twins?"

Mrs. Young smiles at him sweetly, making what my mom calls a bless-your-heart expression. "Bless your heart" is just basically southern for *you're not so bright, but at least you mean well*. "Class, which of y'all can tell us what fraternal twins are?"

Kiera, who is half black and half white with long legs that bump right up against the seat in front of her, raises her hand, her posture perfect, and pulls her hair tie loose, swinging her long braids over her shoulder. Sometimes she seems so pretty and perfect that I feel like I'm watching a movie.

"Yes, Kiera," says Mrs. Young.

"Fraternal twins are twins but don't look exactly alike and sometimes they're boys and girls."

Mrs. Young snaps her fingers. "Eureka!"

"Ohhhhh," says Dusty, giving Kiera the thumbs-up. "Thanks."

"No problem!" she says brightly.

I sigh, but it comes out more like a huff. The worst

part about Kiera is that she's nice. She's just not nice to me, which means that what happened between us is more than just "mean girl drama" as my mom calls it. Because even though I hate to admit it, Kiera's not really a mean girl. In fact, last week she bought lunch for some random fifth grader when their lunch account was at zero.

Kiera shivers and turns around. "Maybe don't breathe down my neck?" She points to my nose. "I think you've got, like, fuzz or a hair in your nose, by the way. Gross."

Red-hot anger blurs my vision. I'm instantly reminded of the first time I spent the night at Kiera's house with her new friends, Sarah Beth, Claire, and Kassidy. I had a stuffy nose, and when I fell asleep, I snored so loud that I even woke myself up. I pretended to still be asleep, though, because all four girls including Kiera were sitting up in a circle, laughing hysterically at me and pretending to snore and drool.

I say nothing back to her. I've made the mistake of responding too soon when someone says something rude, and I just end up sounding ridiculous with an awful comeback like *Shut your butt, Kiera.* That definitely didn't come out as cool as I'd hoped. I always come up with amazing comebacks . . . ten minutes too late. It's my greatest strength and my greatest weakness.

When no one's looking, I brush my finger against my nostrils, careful not to look like I'm picking my nose. Trust me. You don't want to be the kid who gets caught picking their nose in class. I glance behind me and one row over to where Joseph "Digging for Gold" Russo sits. A black boy with electric-blue glasses that I've always thought were super cool, he got caught picking his nose back in third grade, and his life hasn't been the same since.

As I pull my hand back, I sense a light tickling sensation inside my nostril, and I think it might be time for an internet search on how to get rid of nose hair.

CHAPTER FOUR

AKA Patricia

After school, Oscar comes over to Mom's house so we can commence our after-school routine: pretending to do homework while we watch our favorite TV show, *America's Most Haunted*, which has been off the air for something like ten years. Dad says they used to have new episodes every day, and it was even on TV when he and Mom were kids, so we've been working our way through every season on Netflix. We've made it through seven seasons so far and have gotten approximately 4 percent of our homework done during this time. Dad says we're procrastinating. I say it's part of our creative process.

"I can't believe that Lizzie Borden episode last week,"

says Oscar. "Who in the world would want to stay in a bed-and-breakfast inside that woman's house?"

I laugh as I remember Oscar shrieking at the end of the episode when Cliff VanWarren, the show's host, an older white man with a square jaw, what Mom calls a "prominent" nose, and shiny black hair, climbed into bed in the same room where Lizzie supposedly became the first female ax murderer. Cliff winked at the camera and said, "Good night. Sleep tight," and then blew out the one lone candle sitting on the bedside table. Oscar and I both had mega goose bumps.

As we walk down the sidewalk from the bus stop, Oscar teeters around every little crack.

"Someday you're going to step on one," I say.

"You're just jealous of my excellence," he says, and points past my yard to Miss Flora Mae's house. "Whoa. I didn't think she ever even left her house."

I look up and hold my hand above my eyes to shield myself from the sun. "She leaves her house," I tell him. "She checks her mail every night." I've spent a lot of time watching Miss Flora Mae, and even though we've only spoken a dozen or so times, she interacts with me more than she does with just about anyone else in this town. If you ask me, that makes me an expert on all things Miss Flora Mae. That, and I haven't missed a single one of her *Miss Flora Mae I?* letters since I learned how to read.

"Who checks their mail at night?"

"I don't know. People who work during the day?"

"And vampires," he says.

"Well, she's not burning to a crisp, is she?"

But he's got a point. Not a soul on this street has ever seen Miss Flora Mae outside of her house in broad daylight. The closest she gets is her little makeshift screened-in porch, where she taps away on her typewriter. But here she is in a black lace muumuu and a black wide-brimmed sun hat and black cat-eye sunglasses with her gold reading glasses hanging from a strand of beads around her neck.

"Do you think she was the first goth?" asks Oscar. "Like ever?"

"I don't know if she's that hip, but maybe."

Miss Flora Mae didn't always wear all black. Dad said before I was born, when Nana was still her neighbor, she wore a lot more normal clothes. But that was before her husband died.

"Hi, Miss Flora Mae!" I call, mostly to make Oscar squirm.

She startles and then whips around, searching for the source of the sound.

"Over here!" I wave from the sidewalk, moving just past our mailbox. Oscar hangs back, but I yank his arm and wave it in the air along with mine.

"Oh, Patricia!" she says.

Oscar snickers. Sweet Pea might be a sort of ridiculous nickname, but somehow, I find my real name even more embarrassing. The first time I ever spoke with Miss Flora Mae and introduced myself as Sweet Pea, she was quick to say she wasn't a fan of my nickname and would rather call me by my birth name, because she says nicknames should have good backstories, and mine isn't very memorable. The only history on my nickname is that my dad started calling me his Sweet Pea when I was just a baby, and it sort of stuck. Even with my teachers. Nothing funny or epic about that, so to Miss Flora Mae, I'm just Patricia.

"Patricia, dear, come here."

"Be right back," I tell Oscar.

"Squawk like a bird if you need rescuing," he mutters.

I wave a hand in his face to shut him up.

"I've got a favor to ask you," says Miss Flora Mae as she ducks into her garage.

There goes my afternoon of TV and groaning about homework. Mom and Dad would kill me if they knew I said no to our lifelong neighbor during her time of need. At least that's one thing they can still agree on.

My eyes adjust to the darkness of the garage as I walk out of the sunlight to find Miss Flora Mae packing her black Cadillac to the gills. "Whoa! Are you going somewhere?"

To be totally honest, Miss Flora Mae leaves her house so rarely that I forgot what kind of car she even had. Even her groceries are delivered to her. Not with some fancy app or anything, like Aunt Cheryl has in Phoenix, but Green's Grocers does home delivery for senior citizens and people who have trouble leaving their house. Mom says it's that kind of watch-out-for-your-neighbor attitude that she likes about Valentine.

She shakes her head and removes her sunglasses. I notice for the first time how long and smooth her white hair is, parted at the center of her head. "My baby sister, Gloria, has fallen ill." She turns to me. "No matter how old we get she'll always be the baby, so I'm gonna head off to take care of her for the next few weeks."

"I didn't know you had a sister" is all I manage to blurt out. This lady is one giant mystery, but for some reason the thing that shocks me most is that she has any family at all.

She shrugs, tossing an old toolbox into her back seat and then throwing a quilt in after that. The car is full of odds and ends—definitely not the kind of stuff I'd take with me on a road trip to see family. Though the last time we visited Aunt Cheryl, I somehow thought I needed to bring the encyclopedia set Dad got me for Christmas, Mom's old cell phone that she'd passed down to me (not connected, for the record), and three whoopee cushions. Just in case. It was the first time Mom let me pack myself for a trip. (I have to be totally honest and admit that I forgot to pack any underwear. I knew I was forgetting something.)

"Well," she says, "we don't like each other much, but we are cursed to love each other."

I almost gasp. I can't believe she'd have the guts to say something like that out loud—especially to me. Adults are never that honest with kids—but maybe that's what happens when you get old. I've got to say, though, something about the way Miss Flora Mae says things really makes stuff click for me sometimes. Because the way she feels about her sister is pretty much how I'm feeling about my parents right about now: 150 percent cursed.

"So, listen here, Patricia. Mr. Joe Salazar, the newspaper editor, leaves the letters for the advice column in my mailbox three times a week. I try to keep him to a schedule, but I've had no luck taming that man. I'm not real keen on people knowing I'm leaving town, so you keep this between me, you, and your cat, ya hear? Not even your nosy friend."

"Oscar isn't—" Okay, well maybe he is a little bit nosy. "Won't the whole neighborhood see you driving out of town anyway?"

She tosses one single rain boot onto the pile in her back seat. I can't help but wonder where the heck the other one is. "Not if I leave under the cover of darkness, they won't."

I wonder how she got to be this weird, or if she just always was and her husband's death made things worse.

32

"Okay, but what do you need from me?"

"Simple. Gather up my letters and send them to me at my sister's house." She stuffs a crumpled-up piece of scratch paper into the palm of my hand. "Share this address with no one."

"Um . . . okay?"

"Then you check my mail every day, and when I send the letters back with my responses, I just want you to package 'em up all nice in the big envelopes I've left for you in my oven."

"In your oven?" I can't believe I'm hearing right.

"I hate repeating myself, Patricia. It's a true waste of both our time. Leave the answered letters in the mailbox. Joe will come by and get them, and no one will be the wiser. When I get back, as long as you've done what I've asked you, I'll compensate you for your time."

"Compensate me for my time?"

"Again, here we go with the repeating. I. Will. Pay. You. Patricia," she says nice and slow. I must still look pretty confused, because she adds, "With money! Ya know? The green stuff. What did you think I meant?"

I shrug. Sometimes when old people talk about money, they don't get that things aren't as cheap as they used to be. Like, I can't do anything with a dime! Mr. Russo, the gas station clerk at Phillip's Fill 'Em Up and Joseph

"Digging for Gold" Russo's dad, always lets me take a piece of change out of the take-a-penny-leave-a-penny jar at his register like it's some kind of big deal. And I appreciate the thought, but what can I even buy with a penny? Dad says the penny is a drain on the economy and that we should just stop using them. So when Miss Flora Mae says she's going to pay me, I'm not expecting a whole lot of anything.

Heck, when I fed Miss Dillon's cat for a week when she went on a cruise, she told me she'd pay me too. She just didn't say it would be in seashells she'd found on the beach and painted herself. When one of them started stinking up my room, Dad found a dead snail inside. Mom said it was a good lesson in doing nice things without expecting anything in return. I thought it was a good lesson in why you should check your seashells for living creatures before taking them home.

"Miss Flora Mae?" I ask.

"Yes?"

"Why not just mail them back and forth directly from the newspaper?"

She drapes one arm over her car door.

"Patricia, I am a very specific person who wants things done a very specific way, and to be perfectly honest, I owe you no explanation. Now, are you going to help me out or not?"

I gulp. "Okay."

She narrows her eyes. "And this will stay between you and me?"

"Well, and Cheese."

"Who?"

"My cat. Cheese. You did say I could tell my cat."

"Right, right. You, me, and Cheese." She holds her hand out for me to shake. "What an absurd name for a cat."

Way to rub it in, lady.

Miss Flora Mae removes one single key from her key ring and hands it to me. "Guard this with your life, girl."

I nod.

"And if you could water my plants as well."

"Sure thing. Have a safe trip!" I turn to head back down the driveway to rejoin Oscar.

"Talk to 'em too!" calls Miss Flora Mae. "Just tell them about your day. Maybe play them some music. They like the jazz hour on WHPQ. And Aretha. They just swoon for Aretha Franklin."

I twirl back around, my expression totally blank.

"The Queen of Soul!" she says, like I've just taken the Lord's name in vain.

I nod slowly. "Gotcha. The plants. Talking. Music. Jazz. Queen of Soul."

I walk back to where Oscar waits outside the gate to my mom's house.

"What was all that about?" he asks.

I give him a deathly serious look. "I'd have to kill you if I told you." But then I can't contain the laughter that bursts out. "Nothing," I say. "Just weird-old-lady stuff."

Oscar rolls his eyes. "You get all the luck. My next-door neighbor just listens to talk radio really loud and shouts at the raccoons that get into his trash."

CHAPTER FIVE

One Size Does Not Fit All

When Mom gets home from work, she offers to let Oscar stay over for dinner, even though dinner is just frozen lasagna.

Dad is kind of a snob when it comes to pasta, pizza, and cheese because I guess Italian people are supposed to be like that. Dad grew up in Bridgeport, Connecticut. Mom was in her last year of school when Dad was hired to paint the house she was renting. Dad kept messing up the job over and over again until he worked up the courage to ask her out. The rest was history. They got married and moved back to Valentine. I've only visited Connecticut a few times, but I know Dad must have loved Mom to move so far away.

Living in West Texas doesn't leave Dad with many good options for Italian food, so any time it was Mom's turn to cook, she'd make a frozen lasagna, and he'd make this whole show of turning his nose up and pretending like it was beneath him. They'd tease each other back and forth, and it would usually end in Dad stealing a kiss from Mom. It was totally gross, but it was kind of awesome, too, I guess. One time, though, I caught him eating the leftovers in the middle of the night while I was getting a glass of water.

"I thought you hated that stuff," I told him as I rubbed my eyes.

"Can you keep a secret?" he asked.

I sat down at the kitchen table and nodded.

"Sometimes I think I like this stuff better than your own grandmother's sauce, and you better take that to the grave, Sweet Pea."

He handed me a forkful and I took it, even though I'd brushed my teeth hours ago.

"I blame your mother." Dad shook his head. "My mom was right. 'That woman will ruin you,' she said. I just didn't think she'd ruin my refined taste buds."

Oscar and I sit at the kitchen table with our chairs scooted close together while he calls his mom and holds the phone between for both of us to hear.

"Mama, Sweet Pea's mom invited me to stay for dinner."

"Not tonight, baby," she says.

I can't help but blurt, "Nooooooo," and then clap my hand over my mouth as I remember Mrs. Rivera can hear me.

"Moooooom," moans Oscar.

"Don't 'Mom' me. Your father came home early from work and has been working hard trying to figure out my directions for enchiladas for a nice family dinner. Sweet Pea, I love you, but I love the thought of not having to cook a family dinner even more." She pauses. "And yes, I can hear you."

"Hi, Mrs. Rivera," I say, my voice slinking.

"I'll be home soon," Oscar says.

"Music to my ears," she says, and hangs up.

Oscar shrugs. "I tried."

"Maybe next time," I say as he gathers up his stuff and heads out.

In the kitchen, Mom eyeballs the frozen lasagna as she pours hot water on it from the tap, trying to get it to defrost. "How is it that frozen lasagna takes over an hour to cook? Who wants to wait that long for dinner?" She turns the handle on the faucet. "What do you say we head to the mall to grab a bite to eat and then shop for your graduation dress?"

"I'd say, 'Can we get a pretzel after dinner?' and 'Let me get my shoes.'"

We settle on tacos and elotes from Taco Regio and agree

we'll get cinnamon-sugar pretzels after dress shopping. Before we go, Mom wraps her soft brown waves into a low bun and puts on the white linen blazer she wore to work. Dad used to always poke fun at her for wearing her work clothes out around town, like she might be embarrassed if a client saw her without her usual blazer and bun—the true signs that she means business.

After dinner, on our way to Levine's, Mom says, "I got an email from Coach Jeffers. He said you weren't feeling well during PE. You look just fine to me."

"It was just a short stomachache."

With her eyes still on the road, she touches the back of her hand to my head. "Is it your lady time?" she asks, her voice low.

I roll my eyes. "Mom."

She throws her hands up. "You can't blame a mother for wanting to be in tune with her daughter's body."

My whole face turns redder than a tomato. "Uh. Yeah, Mom. You can. That's so weird."

"We don't talk about bodies enough." She rolls her eyes. "A whole country full of people scared of their own bodies. I won't have it. Not my daughter."

I started my period last summer, and the worst part is how weird it makes my mom. She talks about it all the time! I wish it was like in spy movies when I see people leave stuff, like disguises or emergency supplies, in a secret place for other spies to find. Can't she just leave "feminine products" in the cabinet under the sink and never speak of it again? A sudden horror claws at me as I realize I'm going to have to tell Dad to add period supplies to his grocery list now that I have two houses.

Mom sighs with a huff as she realizes the topic isn't really up for discussion. "Did you and Dad read Miss Flora Mae's column this morning?"

"Wouldn't miss it."

"I swear," she says, "that woman is the only reason people still subscribe to that paper."

Mom's not wrong. Miss Flora Mae might be a little nutty in real life, but her advice column is always spot-on. She answers everything from really personal questions to tips and tricks for homemade cleaning products and how to make the perfect peach tea. The woman's advice is basically the next-best thing to the internet. "The only part of the paper I read," I tell her.

"That 'Mom on a Mission' letter was really something," she says.

And my heart deflates a little as I realize that this morning Mom didn't have anyone to read the paper with, because this morning Mom was all on her own.

We park, and as we get out of the car, a gust of warm

wind whips through the parking lot—the promise of a desert thunderstorm rolling through.

Mom's clothes billow in the wind. She always likes wearing all white and lots of flowy linen, because of the heat. Normally something about the way her clothes blow in the wind makes her look so carefree. But not today. Mom's real good at being positive all the time, but I know her well enough to see that she hasn't been the same over the last few months.

Inside Levine's, Mom and I scour every single rack for a dress that I can wear to primary-school graduation. Valentine is such a small town that instead of having elementary, middle, and high schools, we have primary school, which is kindergarten to seventh grade, and then we have secondary school, which is eighth through twelfth grade.

I'm pretty set in my ways when it comes to my wardrobe, but being on the bigger end of the juniors' department means that I don't always have the luxury of being choosy, and that's never more obvious than when I need dress-up clothes. It's like the universe is trying to tell fat people not to bother looking nice. If I'm lucky, I'll find a dumpy floral dress or two, but if I wanted to look like wallpaper . . . I would wear wallpaper.

After endless searching, Mom and I regroup in front of a table of folded tank tops with witty sayings on them in sparkly letters.

"No luck?" Mom asks.

I shake my head. "You?"

She holds up a pair of black stretchy pants and a shirt that I think might actually be a painting smock.

I snarl.

She blows a raspberry. "You're right."

"I like one dress," I tell her, pointing over my shoulder to a black-and-white-striped dress with red, pink, and yellow roses scrawled over the stripes, almost like they were hand painted.

"Maybe they have it in the back," she says, even though the both of us know the answer to that question.

"Let's just go," I beg.

"Let me just ask."

"Mom, please." Not now.

I shake my head again, but Mom's already charging toward the counter at the center of the juniors' department. She dumps the reject items on the counter and rings the bell, prompting the woman behind the counter to turn around.

"Oh!" the woman emits at the sound of the bell. She's tall with wide, round eyes and board-straight red hair. Her freckles are faint and spare across her pale cheeks. Something tells me she's never had to ask if a dress her size was hiding in the back room of the store.

Mom squints at her name tag. "Judith?" She smiles

warmly, turning on her therapist charm. "Judith, how are you on this fine day?"

The woman nods, a little stunned, like that somehow answers Mom's question.

Mom nods back. "Yes, well, you see, my daughter and I were admiring that black-and-white dress with the roses." She points past where I stand, trying to camouflage myself in a rack of swimsuit cover-ups. "Could you please tell me where we can find that dress in a juniors' size eighteen?"

"Just a moment," Judith says as she scurries over and grabs a dress off the rack. She holds it to her chest as she returns to the counter and scans the tag.

I know how this will end, and still my stomach twists into knots as Judith's expression falls into a pout. My cheeks flush as I press my sweaty palms against my sides.

"Hmm," she says.

In my head, I beg her to whisper as she breaks the news so that no one else around her will hear. Not only do I have to face the embarrassment of the store not carrying my size, but I know that my mom will not take it well.

Still, Judith fails to catch my brain transmission as she announces clearly enough for every shopper to hear, "I'm sorry, we don't carry that size in the juniors' department. You'll have to check the regular women's department or the plus-size department." She points to a section behind me, and I don't have to turn around to know it's mostly muumuus and sweatpants.

Mom's shoulders rise and fall as her nostrils flare. I swear the woman breathes fire when she wants. "And why isn't the dress made in a size eighteen, Judith?" Mom asks, overenunciating her name. "Because society has taught us that there's no use in dressing bigger bodies in beautiful clothes, because we do not value bodies of all shapes and sizes. And you want to know who's fed that lie to society?"

I can feel a small crowd gathering as everyone in the juniors' section holds their breath.

Mom doesn't give poor Judith with her perfectly numbered freckles and big, wide saucer eyes a moment to answer. "The patriarchy!" Mom's voice echoes.

Mom whirls around and takes my hand as she drags me to customer service. Without even taking a breath, Mom requests to speak to the manager and the man behind the counter doesn't say no, because it's not very easy to say no to fire-breathing mom dragons.

Mom's the kind of person who truly believes that it's always possible to make things better. She writes letters to the newspaper when they misreport something. And she's known to show up to town-hall meetings to make her opinion heard, because, as she puts it, the meetings wouldn't be open to the public if they didn't want to hear from us.

The manager, a bald man with a thick black mustache,

shuffles out of his office, and Mom lets loose.

She lectures him for what feels like thirty minutes on their failure to stock merchandise for all their customers and the message that sends to people, especially people with larger bodies. The only sign of life from the store manager is the fact that he's still standing and blinks every once in a while.

All the while, I sit slumped on a bench. I wonder what Miss Flora Mae would do or what she would say. I can't help but think that Mom is right. Not having my size in the juniors' department does make me feel like this whole store is one giant party and I'm not invited. It's like when Oscar and I didn't fit into the one-size-fits-all holiday recital robes that the school reuses every year.

I try not to cry, but I can't stop a few of the tears. Mom and Dad have always made it a point to tell me that my body is perfectly fine the way it is. *You only get one body*, Mom says, *and it's a very good body*. They even got in a fight with Coach Jeffers once when he mentioned at a parent-teacher conference that I should work out more. But sometimes no matter how hard I try to remember that I'm just fine the way I am, my head gets the best of me.

Outside the store we sit down on a bench. Mom sheds a couple tears, too, and I know it's not because she's ashamed of me or anything like that. It's because both of us have this habit of feeling things—good and bad—so much that

46

all we can do is cry. And nothing's worse than crying when you're trying to yell at someone.

"Mom?" I ask.

"Yes, Sweet Pea," she says.

"What's the patriarchy?"

She lets out a huge belly laugh. "Oh, baby. I'll tell you another day. I don't want to ruin your day any more than it already has been. Now, we're still on for those pretzels, right?"

"We better be."

Dear Miss Flora Mae,

At the playground yesterday, all the third-grade girls stood around and grabbed their tummies to see how much fat they could fit in their hand. I didn't want to. But they were all looking at me. So I did it, but I needed two hands. Everyone laughed. My best friend didn't.

Why can't I look like them? Mom says everybody has a different body. But who gets to decide what is different and what is not?

Sincerely,
Two Handfuls of Fat

CHAPTER SIX

The Difference Between Like and Like-Like

Since Miss Flora Mae didn't say when her editor, Mr. Salazar, would be dropping off her letters, I decide to make a habit of checking her mail every day just to be extra thorough. There's something sort of exciting about it. We never get anything good in the mail. Or at least I don't.

On Tuesday at lunch, Oscar and I look for a place where both of us can sit together. We pass a table where Alyssa Chang, Samantha Powell, and Tyler Morales sit. Samantha, who is short and about my size with defined curves and milky white skin, whispers to Tyler, who is Mexican and has short curly hair and a light complexion with a few acne scars on his chin. Alyssa, a tall Chinese girl with long black hair twisted into a neat braid, waves Oscar over.

Oscar waves back. "There's only one seat open at your table, and me and Sweet Pea want to sit together."

Alyssa, Samantha, and Tyler all give me the same dry smile.

"Your Christmas-pageant friends don't like me," I say as soon as we're out of earshot.

Oscar rolls his eyes. "They just don't get people who aren't into theater like they are."

"Or they're trying to steal you away from me?" I say, sort of, but not really, joking.

Oscar laughs. "I'm not a car. I can't be stolen, Sweet Pea." He points to the other side of the cafeteria. "Found a spot. Follow me."

Against my better judgment, I follow Oscar and squeeze into the end of a lunch table beside Greg Gunther with his messy blond hair and black rimmed glasses. *Oh, great.* My stomach twists into a knot. I nearly yank Oscar over to a spot next to Safiyah Nazir, a short girl with medium brown skin who always wears the funkiest head scarfs, but I don't move fast enough and the seat is taken. Greg Gunther it is.

Greg Gunther, a tall white boy who's about as wide as a green bean, moved here halfway through the school year, and his arrival was the most exciting thing to happen to our grade since the class pet snake, Goober, went missing and was found in Alyssa's cubby, coiled inside her rain boots.

Meeting Greg made me feel like my stomach was full of hummingbirds. Every night I'd go to sleep and pray that I'd wake up and the feeling would magically disappear in the same way I used to hope for green eyes, like Cheese's.

I didn't know how to describe my feelings until one day after school, while the opening credits of *America's Most Haunted* played on my TV, Oscar turned to me and said, "Truth or dare."

"What?"

"Truth or dare," he demanded again.

I paused the TV, freezing Cliff VanWarren so he looked like a neighing horse. "Dare."

Oscar groaned, and scooted down the couch toward me. "I totally thought you'd go for truth."

I grinned. "That's why I chose dare."

"Okay, fine," he said. "I dare you to tell me if you have a crush on Greg Gunther."

A quick heat danced across my cheeks and down my neck, turning my chest a bright red. My thoughts in exactly this order were: *Gross! Rude! Okay . . . maybe not that gross*. I didn't *like-like* Greg, but even if I did, I knew he wouldn't like a round girl with a surprising amount of body hair.

But my next thought was something I said out loud before I had a chance to decide if it was even a good idea. "Why? Do you like Greg?"

Oscar scoffed, but I know my question wasn't totally out of left field. I was pretty sure Oscar liked boys too.

He looked at me for a while, and I thought he might say more, but instead Oscar patted my knee and said, "Don't worry. That big-nosed goofball is all yours."

I sighed at the thought of Greg and his toothy grin. He was somehow both cool and nerdy at the same time. I slithered down into the cushions of the couch and covered my blushing face with a throw pillow.

"Oh, Sweet Pea," Oscar said dramatically. "Your secret is safe with me." And then he hit play, unfreezing Cliff VanWarren, and life as usual resumed.

As I sit down at lunch with Oscar and open my lunchbox, Greg says, "Sweet Pea would know."

I don't know what he thinks I could possibly know, but that doesn't stop me from grinning like a dweeb, until I catch myself and suddenly stop.

"Sweet Pea would know what?" asks Oscar as he swaps me one tamale for half a peanut butter and banana sandwich. (It's a pity trade, honestly. Oscar's mom's tamales are so good, she makes them every December and lets us sell them at the holiday market for a class fund-raiser.)

"About that Miss Flora lady on your street," says Greg.

Cooper Lawson leans around the other side of Greg.

Coop is a thin black boy with midnight colored skin who always wears his perfectly maintained cowboy hat and creased Wranglers to school no matter how hot it is. He laid claim to Greg on his first day. Oscar says it's like he peed on him to mark his territory. It was kind of annoying the way Cooper hogged Greg, but honestly, if you're lacking in the friend department here in Valentine, the only option is to act fast when fresh meat shows up.

"My brother, Dale, said she keeps every single one of her pets that die and gets them stuffed at Topher's Taxidermy on Eleventh Avenue. But that's not the weirdest part. She captures any mice in her house and gets them stuffed and uses them to re-create famous paintings."

"I don't actually—"

"Sweet Pea is, like, the only person Miss Flora Mae even talks to," says Oscar, like that's suddenly something worth bragging about.

Way to put me on the spot. "Not true. She talks to other people."

"Well, you live next to her, don't you?" asks Greg.

"More like she lives on either side of her," says Oscar. Immediately, he realizes he's said too much and looks at me in a panic. Mom and Dad getting a divorce was sort of big news here in town. No one really knows *why* they got a divorce, but it's not every day that the town therapist, who is known for her marital counseling, gets a divorce herself. That's scandal enough without people knowing they're basically neighbors now.

"Huh?" grunts Cooper. "What does that even mean?"

I let out a puff of air. "My mom lives on one side of her house and my dad lives on the other."

"Whoa," says Greg. "That's so weird." But he doesn't say it in a mean way. More like when you find out that narwhals are real or that the heart of the shrimp is located in its head. "Are you excited about double Christmases and double birthdays?" he asks.

"Yeah," says Cooper. "I've always been kind of jealous of kids with divorced parents. Double gifts. Double allowance. Double vacation."

I stare down at my half sandwich and tamale, considering where to start. "It's really not that great," I mumble.

"Sweet Pea," says Greg, "I meant to tell you, I found this YouTube channel that's nothing but *America's Most Haunted* Easter eggs and conspiracy theories."

"Oh, cool," I say. And then trying to sound very casual, "Maybe you can show us during our library hour?"

I thought maybe once I got to know Greg, the anxious feelings would go away, but it only made it worse. He loves my and Oscar's favorite TV show, and every time he and his family go on vacation, they do whatever ghost tour is local to that city, so he's, like, very cultured. He's even gone on a cemetery tour in New Orleans. And on top of all that, he has two cats. A boy cat person! They're both fat tabbies (one with a stubby tail) who lived in the dumpster behind his uncle's Cajun restaurant in Houston. Their names are Gumbo and Beignet—how cute is that?

Greg's eyes shine as he continues. "One guy thinks Cliff VanWarren isn't even alive and that he's actually a ghost. Like, that he died during filming in an early season and his spirit still hosted the show until it was canceled."

Did I mention that he's not even a little bit ashamed of looking like a big nerd? I like people who like the things they like, even when others don't get it.

Oscar gasps. "You don't think it was the episode on Mackinac Island, do you? When he fell down that rocky hill?"

Greg thinks about that for a minute and then nods. "Totally possible! I mean, it sounds unbelievable, but if you look at the evidence—"

"Hey!" says Cooper, clearly annoyed. "What about Kiera's party at Trampoline Zone this Sunday? That's going to be awesome. I can't believe her dad got them to let her have a party there two whole weeks before they open."

Kiera's having a birthday party? I feel queasy. "Yeah," I squeak. "I think I've got something else going on that weekend."

Greg whispers something to Cooper, and all I can make

out is the word *invited*. I shrink back a little, completely mortified. The only thing worse than realizing you've been left out is when other people know you've been left out.

Last year, Kiera went on a big trip to New York City for her birthday, and the year before that she had a slumber party with her other friends, Sarah Beth, Kassidy, and Claire, so this is the first year I've had to face the reality of her having a big birthday party and not inviting me. I feel sick to my stomach, and I hate that I care so much, because that means, somewhere deep down, Kiera still has the power to hurt my feelings.

What else did I expect, though? And of course she's having it at Trampoline Zone, the place everyone in Valentine under the age of fourteen has been waiting months for. Oscar and I watched with eyes bigger than avocados as they started doing construction on the Valentine Mini Mall Shopping Center months ago.

Oscar looks at me, his face ashen with embarrassment, and I don't have to be a detective to know that even he got an invite. I bite my lips together, keeping my anger bottled up. He could've at least warned me!

I eat the rest of my lunch in silence while Greg and Cooper talk about our end-of-year field day and all the ridiculous pranks Coop wants to play on the sixth graders before we leave this place behind for secondary school.

If I could get over my own little pity party, I would talk to them about how weird it is that at Valentine Primary School, we're treated like royalty, because we're finally the oldest.

Honestly, the secondary school is just across the street, but I still don't like to think about graduating, since we're basically the seniors of primary school right now. In secondary school we're just going to be starting at the bottom of the food chain all over again. And by the looks of it, I'll be at the bottom of the bottom all by myself.

That afternoon, as I'm walking to my bus, Oscar calls out to me. "Sweet Pea! Wait up!"

I don't turn around. I'm trying to decide if I'm still mad at him. It sure feels like it.

"Come on! You know I hate running," he says in between pants as he skids to a stop a few feet behind me.

I finally turn around. "You could have told me about Kiera's party."

His shoulders slump. "It's not like I would go without you. Even if I would sell my baby cousin for a chance to go to Trampoline Zone a whole two weeks before it opens."

"So you *were* invited?" I squawk.

"I found the invitation in my mailbox last Tuesday," he admits.

I cross my arms over my chest and blink back any stray tears. Valentine Primary School has a rule that if you're going to hand out birthday-party invitations, you have to invite the whole class, so of course Kiera would be clever enough to get around that rule by mailing invites to her guest list. And no offense, but if she invited Oscar, she invited basically everyone. Except me.

I don't even want to open my mouth, because I'm scared that if I do, I might cry. So I just shrug and wave to Oscar to follow me to the bus.

"You're not even friends with Kiera," I remind him.

"She probably just invited me to annoy you."

"That doesn't help," I say through gritted teeth.

"We'll have our own dang party," he says. "Me, you, Cheese, and some R-rated movies from my brother's stash."

Oscar's my best friend, and I think I would actually die without him, but part of me will always miss Kiera and our Saturday mornings in the bowling alley arcade.

My earliest memories of hanging out with Kiera are from the bowling alley. Our dads would meet for bowling league, and Kiera and I would find ourselves lumped together. It wasn't friendship at first sight or anything. She liked sitting there on her dad's knee when it wasn't his turn, and I preferred to get lost in the arcade while I checked every crane machine to make sure someone hadn't accidentally left their prize behind or maybe even a few spare tokens.

It was pure luck when the only time someone actually forgot their crane-machine prize, Kiera was passing through the arcade on her way to the bathroom. I gasped so loudly, she froze right there on the black carpet with neon geometric shapes.

"Is your hand caught?" she asked immediately. Her nose wrinkled up. "Or is it something gross? It's something gross, isn't it? The one time I stuck my hand in one of these things, I found a half-eaten hot dog."

"What do you call a hot-dog competition?" I asked her.

She shook her head. "I don't know, but are you ever going to pull your hand out of that crane machine?"

"Wiener takes all!" I said, and yanked my arm out of the crane machine, my fist clenched around a hot-pink stuffed elephant.

"Oh my gosh! You *found* that?"

She and I spent the rest of the morning checking every machine for tickets, loose change, gumballs, and whatever other treasures we might find. When we came up with nothing else, I offered her the elephant and she took it.

On the way home, I told Dad that I felt bad because I really wanted to keep the elephant and didn't actually want to give it to Kiera, but I felt like the nice thing to do was to at least offer it to her.

"But you gave it to her anyway?" he asked. "Right?"

I nodded. "Well, of course."

"And it didn't feel entirely good?"

I shook my head.

"Sometimes those are the things that mean the most. When we share or give something that is actually hard to part with but do it anyway."

I sighed into my chest and mumbled something about him being right.

"Sounds like you might have gotten something in return, though."

"What's that?"

"A friend," he said.

CHAPTER SEVEN

Good as Gravy

I collapse face-first next to Cheese on the couch, pressing my cheek into his fuzzy belly. He lets out a loud purr, so I give him a good scratch under his chin.

"You sure you don't want to go to Dad's with me?" I ask.

His only response is to paw at my ponytail.

"I'll take that as a no."

I think Cheese's disinterest in staying with me at Dad's might just be the worst part of this whole deal. Mom says I'm too young to be a cat lady, but I think it's too late.

Mom sweeps past me as she slips into a pair of wedges and drops a pile of mail on the counter. "Give this to your father, would you? It's his mail. I promised I'd bring it by before I left for book club, but I completely forgot."

I moan.

She gives me a quick kiss on the forehead, and Cheese swats at her nose.

"Don't forget his mail. There's some important stuff in there. And he's no good at keeping up with papers, anyway."

"Yes, ma'am."

"Sweet Pea," she pauses, waiting for me to look at her.

I sit up and yawn without covering my mouth.

"I know it's been a week full of changes, but I think if we can just get in the swing of this routine, we'll be good as gravy."

I puff out a held breath, blowing my bangs up. It's not that I want my parents to fight and bicker all the time like normal divorced parents, but something about the way they're trying to pretend like nothing has changed makes all of this so much harder. It was never my stupid carpet or my bedspread or my wallpaper that made our house a home. It was us. The three of us plus Cheese.

Nothing about this is as good as gravy.

"Right?" Mom asks.

And I realize she's been waiting this whole time for me to respond. "Right as rain," I mumble.

"How do I look?" she asks, motioning down to her cream sundress and shawl.

"It's just book club. It's not like you're going anywhere special."

The edges of her lips turn down.

"But you look great," I tell her quickly, guilt settling over me. "Really pretty."

"Well, I am meeting a friend afterward for some margaritas and chips and salsa."

"What friend?" I ask. Suddenly something feels weird.

She winks at me. "Call me if you need me, and leave the porch light on when you head over to Dad's."

After she leaves, I putter around the house for a bit with Cheese weaving in and out of my legs like he's either trying to slow me down or trip me. Or maybe he's just trying to get me to stay, which really makes me feel like crud. Finally, I give in and shove Dad's mail in my backpack and head on over. I try to ignore Cheese's soft meow as I make my way down to the sidewalk. If Mom and Dad wanted to keep things so normal, why didn't they just stay married?

On my way there, I take a quick peek inside Miss Flora Mae's mailbox and find it empty. Tomorrow I'll go over and play some music for her plants, which is probably the most ridiculous thing anyone has ever asked me to do, by the way.

"Dad?" I call out as I push his front door open. There's something weird about this place. It's not home enough for me to feel like I can just walk in, but Dad living here also means I feel really silly knocking or ringing the doorbell.

"In here!" he calls from the living room. "What do you think about Frito pie for dinner?"

"I think it sounds like something Mom wouldn't define as dinner."

"Guess it's a good thing Mom's not here," says Dad as he stands up from the single love seat in his living room.

A smile tickles at my lips. "Frito pie it is!"

Dad's Frito pie isn't like normal Frito pie. He makes his tortilla strips himself and keeps frozen batches of his home-made chili in the freezer for whenever the mood strikes. He even shreds my absolute favorite cheddar cheese (other than my cat) made in Tillamook, Oregon.

Dad sets up his TV-dinner trays so we can watch *American Ninja Warrior* while we eat dinner. We eat in silence, adding sprinkles of cheese every time we eat the top layer of chips, chili, and cheese. "Ya gotta make every bite cheesy," says Dad with his mouth full.

I laugh through a huge bite. Dad may never have gone to college, but he's one of the smartest people I know. Besides, Mom always says college isn't for everyone, and it doesn't make you better than anyone else.

As we're finishing, Dad turns to me during a commercial break.

"Hey, uh, did your mom send over any of my mail with you?"

I can't quite explain why, but for some reason I'm in no hurry at all to give Dad his mail. Maybe I'm just annoyed that he can't go over there and get it himself.

"She must have forgotten," I finally say.

Quietly, Dad grunts and then he forces a smile. "No problemo, Sweet Pea. No problemo at all."

CHAPTER EIGHT

By Invitation Only

It's not the last day of school, but with the way people are buzzing over Kiera's birthday party, it sure feels like it. I'm not kidding. I think even the cafeteria ladies were invited.

After lunch, Kiera's mom brings vanilla cupcakes from Blue Bird Bakery that have been clustered together and iced to look like the heart-eyes emoji, everyone's favorite. I think even Mrs. Young is excited.

"It's almost like we get two end-of-the-year parties with Kiera's birthday being so close to summer," I hear someone say while we're in line for cupcakes.

Oscar rolls his eyes. "Blah, blah. All hail Kiera."

I snicker, even though it feels mean.

Kiera stands next to her mom at the front of the

classroom, doling out cupcakes and going out of her way to give the best ones to the other pretty girls, like Alyssa, who is tall and willowy, and Samantha with her curly golden hair.

As we make our way to the front and Kiera hands Oscar a cupcake with yellow icing, I hear her tell her mom, "I asked for the two-tier cake. Everyone gets cupcakes. What's special about cupcakes?"

"Kiera," her mother says through a gritted smile, "cupcakes are easier to serve at school. Besides, cake is cake."

Kiera turns to me and hands me one of the few cupcakes with black icing. Great. That's gonna stain my teeth forever, basically.

"Oh, hi Sweet Pea!" Mrs. Bryant croons. "Will we see you on Sunday at the party?"

"Uh . . ."

"She's busy," says Kiera quickly.

Mrs. Bryant clicks her tongue. "What a shame." She looks at me in earnest. Kiera is beautiful just like her mom. Mrs. Bryant is a petite black woman who wears her hair cut into a short pixie style. Kiera gets her height from her dad, who is a tall white guy with sandy-colored hair and suntanned leathery skin from years spent outside in the oil fields as he worked his way up to an office job. That means he spends most of his weekdays traveling all over the state.

Mrs. Bryant gently reaches for my elbow before I can

slink away. "Is your mother doing okay with . . . with every-thing?"

I nod. "Just fine, Mrs. Bryant." Mom has always liked Mrs. Bryant. She says Mrs. Bryant softens Mr. Bryant's bravado, whatever that means.

"Well, listen," she says, "if you find the time, we'd love to have you at the party."

I turn to Kiera, my gaze narrowed. "I'll talk to my mom."

Class birthday parties are like the wild, wild west where the rules don't apply, so I plop down on top of Oscar's desk, something Mrs. Young—who's doing a little happy dance with her shoulders as she gobbles down her cupcake—would never tolerate during normal classroom time.

I have a staring contest with my cupcake, wondering how bad the damage will be from the black icing.

"It's worth it," Oscar says through a mouthful of cake and icing. "Staining your teeth black is worth it. This stuff is delicious."

I heed his advice and take a giant chomp out of my cupcake. Mrs. Bryant was right. Cake is cake. "Guess who just got invited to Kiera's birthday party?"

He gasps and chokes on a few cupcake crumbs.

I pat his back and nod. "Kiera might just kill her mom for asking me to go." I shrug. "She's got nothing to worry about. I'd never go anyway."

"Or you could," says Oscar, taking a swig of his lemonade. "We both could." It's hard to ignore the hope in his voice. Kiera may not be his biggest fan, but if he skips out on this party, it'll be my fault, not hers.

"I'm not that desperate."

He nudges me. "Forget desperation. What better way to stick it to Kiera than to crash her perfect birthday party?"

If my life was a movie where I always had the best ideas and knew the perfect thing to say, I'd say Oscar was right. But the whole thought of it makes me uneasy. No way am I cool enough to pull off crashing Kiera's birthday party without making myself look like the loser—or even getting kicked out! Talk about mortification to the billionth power.

Something about the whole idea, though, is hard for me to shake. It would be kind of great to go to Trampoline Zone. "I'll think about it."

"Sleepover at your place tonight?" asks Oscar.

"Sure." I polish off the rest of my cupcake and check out my reflection in the window looking out onto the after-school pickup lanes outside. Yup, I look like I just ate a fistful of charcoal right out of the grill.

"Wait," says Oscar. "Your mom's or your dad's?"

"Dad," I say.

Greg walks past us with a cupcake iced with a big heart eye, handpicked by Kiera, I'm sure. He points to his teeth and says, "Zombie teeth. Nice."

"It's the latest trend. It's to die for."

He laughs. "You're pretty funny, Sweet Pea."

Not even the thought of my stained teeth can wipe the smile off my face.

CHAPTER NINE

The Witching Hour

Dad's usually a rule follower, but there are certain things, like scary movies (and *America's Most Haunted*), that he loves so much, he doesn't want to keep them from me. Which is why Oscar and I are curled up beside my dad, watching a movie called *Jaws*. I keep pulling my T-shirt collar up over my eyes. Something about seeing the shark lurk through the filter of my threadbare T-shirt makes this slightly less scary.

"How is this even scary?" I shout over the dramatic music as the shark prepares to attack in the murky waters below an unsuspecting boat.

"I don't know," says Oscar as he takes the popcorn bowl from my dad. "It's not even a real shark. Like, it is so

71

obviously a fake shark. This movie is so old it might as well be in black and white, but—" He shrieks and jumps in his seat, sending the popcorn into the air.

"Oh my god, oh my god. What did I miss?" I ask, my hands safely covering my eyes as the music reaches an ear-splitting pitch.

"What were you saying again?" Dad chuckles. "About this movie being old?"

Oscar huffs. "Well, it's definitely old."

"Still pretty scary, though," says Dad as he plucks a piece of popcorn out of my hair and eats it. "Oscar, am I going to be in trouble with your mom for showing you a scary movie? Your mother is one heck of a lioness."

"My brothers have scarred me for life, so I'm pretty sure you're safe, Mr. DiMarco." Oscar looks around. "Should I get the, uh, vacuum to clean all this up?"

Dad surveys the popcorn damage. "I really need a dog." He shakes his head and crosses his foot over his knee, leaning back into the sofa. "We'll leave it for the morning. Don't want anyone to miss any of the good parts."

"There are good parts in this movie?" I squeak.

Dad puts his arm around me and tugs me closer to him. "I've got a thing or two to teach you yet, Sweet Pea."

I glance around at the popcorn all over the floor and our laps. Mom would freak out, but Mom's not here.

Oscar and I lie in my room all tucked in, him on the air mattress purchased for the camping trip my mom refused to go on, because she has a fear of snakes (I wanted to be annoyed at her for that, but snakes freak me out pretty bigtime too), and me in my bed. Well, my second bed.

There's something about the way the shadows are cast against the wall in this room that makes the whole place feel haunted. I don't actually think there are any ghosts here, but this room reminds me of a bad guy in a crummy disguise. Like, the kind you might see in a cartoon where the bad guy just puts on a fake mustache and a trench coat and somehow manages to fool everyone except me.

Oscar falls asleep first, and then I begin to drift, but only for a moment before my eyes shoot open and I gasp. There's nothing worse than being shocked awake by the realization that you forgot your homework or to clean your cat's litter box. (To be honest, I don't know which of those is worse.)

I was supposed to go over to Miss Flora Mae's today, and I 250 percent forgot. I slide out of bed and tiptoe around a sleeping Oscar. The clock on my bedside table says it's nearly one in the morning—what Cliff VanWarren would call the witching hour. I suck in a deep breath as my bedroom door creaks shut behind me.

Down the hallway, a glowing blue light from the TV leaks out from under the door of Dad's bedroom.

Sometimes Mom would sleep on the couch because she couldn't fall asleep with the TV on and Dad had a hard time falling asleep with it off. Mostly, they'd just set a timer, but now I wonder if Mom sleeping in the guest room wasn't really about the TV.

A little farther down the hallway is Dad's third bedroom. If I weren't on a mission, I might just sneak in there and nose around, but I also kind of feel like if Dad hasn't let me in there, maybe I'm not meant to see what's behind the door.

Carefully, I slide out the front door before I have the chance to think too seriously about the fact that I'm sneaking out in the middle of the night. On the one hand, I feel pretty dang cool, but on the other hand, it kind of freaks me out. Like, what if I'm kidnapped and my parents just think I disappeared?

The streetlamp on the corner flickers before shutting off for the night. I check the mail, holding Miss Flora Mae's key close to my chest as I run up her sidewalk and onto her shadowed porch.

I don't believe in monsters. I don't believe in monsters. I don't believe in monsters. I don't believe in monsters. I don't believe in monsters.

I've never bought into Oscar's theories about Miss Flora Mae, but somehow the wind is howling louder than it should and the porch is creaking with every breath I take and I can't help but feel like I am definitely on an episode of *America's Most Haunted* and somewhere out there Cliff VanWarren is narrating my every move.

No matter how steady I make my hand, I can't seem to get the key in the hole just right. "Come on," I mutter, not willing to look over my shoulder behind me into the dark, whistling wind.

I may not believe in monsters, but I can think of about a billion other things I do believe in. Ghosts, aliens, wild animals, kidnappers . . .

The lock clicks, and short-lived relief washes over me as I step into an even deeper darkness. For a moment, I fumble around, sliding my hands up the walls, looking for a light switch. I run headfirst into what I hope is a lamp and not a dead body just chilling out in the middle of Miss Flora Mae's house for no suspicious reason at all. I pat down the lamp/possible dead body until— "Aha! Let there be light!"

I clap my hand over my mouth, muffling my own scream as my eyes focus on the hissing cat resting on the mantel above the fireplace.

Miss Flora Mae never said anything about a cat!

"Kitty?" I ask very quietly. "Kitty?"

Slowly I approach the Maine Coon cat with a fluffy tuft of white fur around its neck. When it doesn't move, I reach out to touch its paw, prepared to haul butt back to my dad's house. If I die in this house, the only thing Oscar will say at my funeral is, "I told you so." And he won't be wrong.

With one eye closed, I bring my hand down on the cat's very matted paw. "Here, kitty, kitty."

I hold my breath for a whole two seconds . . . and nothing. Not a dang thing happens. Stepping a little closer, I see a small gold plaque that reads *RIP Bette Davis the Cat, 1998–2014*.

A cat. I look up in horror at its glassy eyes. A very dead cat.

I poke it once more to be sure. Yup, still dead.

I look around for more stuffed dead animals. I've seen people mount deer or even birds they hunted, but I've never heard of someone actually stuffing their dead pet to keep forever. That gives me the heebie-jeebies, but I think more than that, it makes me sad.

There are posters from old movies and a few framed records from some people I recognize, like Dolly Parton and Aretha Franklin, who I remember Miss Flora Mae mentioning, but others I've never heard of, like Stevie Nicks, Etta James, Billie Holiday, Ella Fitzgerald, and Janis Joplin. A thin layer of dust coats the stacks of art books on her coffee table, and by the looks of it two people named Richard Avedon and Georgia O'Keeffe are her favorites.

I peek out into her sunroom, which is a small

screened-in part of her porch you can only get to from inside the house. Her typewriter sits there by itself, and on her chair is a thick manila envelope with a note on top that says *TO: PATRICIA*. Carefully, I open the envelope and slide out a piece of paper addressed to me.

Dear Patricia,

This is my first batch of letters that Mr. Joe Salazar will be picking up for the paper. The letters should be left in my mailbox no later than Tuesday afternoon. In my kitchen, inside the utensil drawer, you'll find a roll of stamps. Please put the letters left in my mailbox by Mr. Joe Salazar in a large envelope (find those inside the oven, where I keep important documents) and post them to me at my sister's address.

DON'T. FORGET. TO. WATER. MY. PLANTS. And jazz music! Aretha! Talk radio causes them to wither—as it does to any living thing.

Sincerely,
Miss Flora Mae

I take the note and letters with me as I make my way into the kitchen, which is stocked with every type of canned food imaginable. When the zombie apocalypse strikes, I know where Cheese and I are going. It's like the lady has stashed as many things as possible in her house so that she never has to leave.

The oven is stuffed with important papers, just like the note promised, but it's actually kind of organized in here. If I weren't still spooked, I might get a little nosy and dig around.

After guessing how many stamps I might need, I give the plants a quick watering (the music will have to wait) and lock up the front door as quickly as I can and run out to the mailbox with two large envelopes of letters in my hands—one is unanswered mail to be sent to Miss Flora Mae and the other is answered letters for Mr. Joe to publish in next week's paper. Just as I open the mailbox, a single letter falls out.

I reach down to grab it, thinking maybe it's just a piece of regular mail. But when I hold it under the moonlight, all I see is a totally blank envelope sealed with a sparkling heart sticker. I put the answered and unanswered letters in the mailbox, but I hold on to this loose one for a moment, trying to decide what to do with it, before shoving it in the pocket of my pajama pants. I don't even have to read it, I tell myself. I'll just hold on to it until I go back to Miss Flora Mae's. Save myself a trip back into the house.

I close the door on the mailbox with the two envelopes of letters inside, and I jog back over to Dad's house with the one stray envelope burning a hole in my pocket.

Before I go inside, I glance over to Mom's house. From her bedroom window, I can see Cheese's silhouette in a glowing blue light. I guess Mom left her TV on too.

CHAPTER TEN

100% Duck

I can barely contain my excitement as I wiggle my way back into my bedroom, where Oscar is still sound asleep. I definitely have no business reading someone else's mail, but one little peek can't hurt.

Just as I'm about to be home free, my mattress squeaks as I lie down.

"Sweet Pea?" asks Oscar, his voice slow and sleepy.

"I just went to get some water," I tell him.

"Mmmm. I'm thirsty."

"I left my cup in the kitchen."

"Root beer floats," he says, his voice higher than normal, like he's caught somewhere between a dream and reality.

"Strawberry milkshakes." He smacks his lips together and promptly falls back into a deep sleep.

I reach for the mini flashlight in my nightstand, then wait a few moments until his breathing hits a rhythm and I know for sure he's out.

I pull the covers up over my head and even throw my pillow over myself to dim the glow of the flashlight. I'm careful to open the letter along the seal without ripping the envelope or sticker. I unfold a piece of paper taken out of a spiral notebook, but with the loose edges torn neatly off.

Dear Miss Flora Mae,

I'm not a big fan of asking for help. Honestly, I didn't even buy into the whole Santa thing, so writing letters to some random person I've only heard of and never met really isn't my style, if you get what I mean.

But I'm stuck in a big way. My parents are pretty good at being parents. Sometimes my mom is annoying and asks too many questions, and sometimes my dad doesn't ask enough and works too much, but lately they've been fighting. And my dad is starting to care about things he never cared about before, like how often my mom gets her nails done and how much money my summer camp costs.

You probably think I'm a spoiled brat. I know I'm really lucky, okay? I don't need a lecture about that. But the other night when I was supposed to be asleep, I heard my mom talking about taking a break. Like, from each other. I don't know what to think. It feels like they're lying to me. And that makes me angry, but more than anything, I want things to go back to how they used to be. I'm not asking for the perfect parents or anything. Just for things to go back to normal.

Sincerely,
Not a Spoiled Brat

Under the covers my breath is hot and muggy. I look over the letter once more. Not to read it, but to *look* at it. I would know those little curls at the end of each letter anywhere. Even if we hadn't spent all of first, second, third, and most of fourth grade swapping notes back and forth, I'd know this handwriting just from seeing it every day at school or from the piles of handwritten notes I've seen passed around the classroom.

I scoff. Not a spoiled brat? Yeah, right. When Nana was

still alive, she'd always say, "When people show you who they are, believe 'em! Walks like a duck, talks like a duck. It's a duck."

Glancing down at the letter once more, I feel like I'm holding a ticking bomb and a golden ticket all at once.

I turn off the flashlight and slide the letter under my pillow. I don't know what I'm going to do with it. I know what I *should* do with it. I should run back out to Miss Flora Mae's mailbox first thing in the morning and add it to the bundle of letters headed to her sister's house.

Or I could keep the letter. I could throw it away and make it disappear.

But what if . . . I answered it?

I pull the covers up over my chest and squeeze my eyes shut. Whatever decision I make, I don't think I can make it tonight. But no matter how hard I close my eyes, Kiera Bryant's handwriting is burned into the back of my eyelids like an image I just can't shake.

The next morning, Dad makes Texas-shaped waffles for breakfast.

"Mr. DiMarco," says Oscar, "do you think other states have waffle makers shaped like them?"

Dad laughs. "I think it might just be a Texas thing, buddy." He flips the iron over. "What do you think, SP?"

The letter is just where I left it under my pillow, and it feels like a lit match, just waiting to catch the whole place on fire.

Dad waves his spatula in the air. "SP? Earth to Sweet Pea?"

I snap to attention. "Uh, yeah. Totally."

Dad sets the syrup on the table and squints at me. "You feeling okay?"

"Just still a little tired."

Dad nods, returning to his waffle maker.

Oscar shakes his head. "SP. Not only do you have a nickname, but your nickname has a nickname. I don't even have a nickname to begin with."

I shrug. "My dad's the only one who calls me SP. And only sometimes."

"Oscar Mayer," Dad pipes in. "OM! Ommmmmm," he says like he's meditating.

"Listen, Mr. DiMarco, no offense or nothing, but people at school have enough things to poke fun at without nicknaming me after a hot dog."

Dad chuckles and turns back to his waffle maker. "Roger that."

"Hey, Sweet Pea," Oscar says a little too loudly. "Have you gotten anything for Kiera's birthday party tomorrow?"

Dad turns his head to the side, but with his eyes still on the waffle iron. "Kiera? Little Kiera Bryant? You haven't brought her around in some time now. I didn't know she was having a birthday party."

I open my mouth to explain that I'm not going, because I most definitely was not invited.

"Oh yeah," says Oscar. "A huge party at Trampoline Zone."

"I didn't think that place opened for another few weeks."

"Her parents got the place to let her have her party there anyway."

Dad shakes his head. "Good for Kiera," he says. But I know what he's not saying. Mr. Bryant, who Mom calls a "polarizing personality," and Dad have been friends since Dad moved back here with Mom after she was done with college. Unfortunately for Dad, though, Mr. Bryant didn't take it too well when Dad explained to his bowling team why he and Mom were getting a divorce.

Oscar looks at me meaningfully. He's the only person I've told about Dad, and there's nothing Oscar respects more than a secret, especially one this huge.

"Breakfast is served!" says Dad, placing a plate of waffles in front of us. He claps his hands together. "We'll drop Oscar off and then pick out a present for Kiera's birthday party?"

I look to Oscar. I know he's dying to go to Trampoline Zone, and he was willing to skip the whole thing just for me. If I think about it, I guess I *kind of* was invited. I mean, Mrs. Bryant said so.

I nod. "Okay."

I know it's a bad idea, but something about that letter from last night spurs me to say yes.

CHAPTER ELEVEN

It's the Thought That Counts

When I was little, I used to do this thing when I went shopping for birthday presents where I would just buy all the things that I really wanted that Mom wouldn't let me get for myself. So that meant when Mom wasn't really paying attention, Dusty got a Harry Potter cloak when the only thing he cared about was Pokémon and Alyssa got a water-balloon gun even though she cried when she got her hair wet at field day.

I guess you could say I've grown up a little bit, but sometimes I still love present shopping because it gives me a chance to buy things I think are cool even when I don't get to keep them. But if I'm going to go to the trouble of buying a present for Kiera, I'm at least going to use it as an opportunity, which is why my dad asked me if I was totally 100 percent sure when I skipped up to the register with a lint roller, a book called *The U in Puberty*, and deodorant.

"Sweet Pea," Dad says, eyeing me suspiciously. "That doesn't seem like a very thoughtful gift. What about a game? Or maybe some of that flavored lip gloss you're always asking me for?"

"Trust me," I say. "Kiera will love this. We're both cat lovers." I hold up the lint roller. Which is totally true, actually. Kiera has a tuxedo cat named Domino who has one extra toe on his back left paw. "And one can never have too many lint rollers." I point to the deodorant on the conveyor belt. "This is rose scented. She'll love it. Here, smell it."

Dad pulls back. "Uh, no thanks. I'm good."

I hold up the book. "And Mom is always saying we should all be more in touch with our bodies."

Dad blushes and pulls a gift bag from the display next to the greeting cards. "At least get her a bag and a card."

"Sure thing, Daddio."

As I'm picking out a card and a bag, I remember the letter Kiera wrote, and for a minute I kind of feel a little bad. Parental drama is the worst.

My fingers trail along the cards until they settle on a card shaped like a pickle. The inside reads, "Happy Birthday. I got you this pickle."

"Perfect," I mutter to myself as my guilt dissolves.

In the car, with Dad's pen, I sign the card and add, *Here's a pickle since you decided ours wasn't worth keeping.*

Trust me. To Kiera, it will make sense.

After that first morning at the bowling alley when Kiera and I hung out in the arcade, we started spending more time together. I'll never forget going over to her house for the first time and seeing that elephant from the claw machine given prime real estate front and center on her perfectly made bed.

Pickle the stuffed hot-pink elephant became sort of our friendship mascot. We named him Pickle because we thought it went well with Cheese. After all, cheese and pickles are the most common toppings on any burger. Pickle stayed there at Kiera's house on her bed until the first slumber party she hosted in fourth grade with me and all her new fifth-grade friends, a tight circle of pretty girls, several of whom even had boyfriends. All they talked about was which YouTubers were dating who and which of them had started their periods. I tried to smile along even though I felt totally left out.

"Hey, where'd Pickle go?" I whispered to Kiera when no one else was around.

She shrugged. "Me and my mom cleaned out my room, and I donated him with a bunch of other toys."

My heart sunk to the floor. "You did what?"

"Claire came over." She pointed to the tall white girl

with smooth hair the color of butter who everyone else always seemed eager to impress. Claire stood clustered together with Sarah Beth, a black girl with tight ringlet curls, and Kassidy, a pale girl with orange freckles and reddish brown waves swept into a high ponytail.

Kiera waved to Claire, and all three girls waved back. "She helped me clear out a bunch of old stuff. She's really nice, you know. These girls used to make me so nervous, but they're really cool."

I nodded, not sure what to even say. I couldn't figure out why Kiera was in such a hurry to be older and different . . . and leave me behind. Because I was in no hurry at all. The thought of fifth grade terrified me—not to mention actual fifth graders!

"It's not a big deal," said Kiera, her voice reassuring, but it did nothing to soften the brutal honesty of her words.

It was a big deal. It still is.

CHAPTER TWELVE

Our Very Best Life

When we pull up outside of Trampoline Zone, Oscar is sitting outside on the curb waiting for me with a present stuffed in a reused Spider-Man gift bag.

"You okay if I just drop you off here, Sweet Pea?" asks Dad.

I nod. If it weren't for Kiera's dad, he'd probably go in and talk to the other parents. Part of me wishes I hadn't agreed to go to this party with Oscar and I could just sit in the parking lot with Dad watching all the other kids file in.

"Okay," he says. "Just borrow an adult's cell phone if you need me before the party is over."

"You know, you could just consider giving me a phone a few months early. Why wait for eighth grade to start?"

"Not gonna happen."

"Can't blame me for trying," I tell him as I shut the car door behind me. I turn to Oscar. "Your present looks like it was gift wrapped at Love's Hardware."

"I had to get creative with my supplies." He holds up the present for me to examine. "I used a bag from an old birthday party."

I snort. "Only the best for Princess Kiera."

"I'm surprised you even bought a present."

I can't hide the mischief in my smirk. "The gifts are the best part."

"You're up to something," he says, narrowing his eyes.

Eager to change the subject, I shout, "I challenge you to a duel in the ball pit!"

"Bring. It. On."

We knock on the front door, and a teen boy with light brown skin and black shaggy hair with a name tag reading *Ricky* cracks the door open. "You here for the party?" he asks, like he's gonna ask us for our driver's license or something.

"Yup," I tell him, waving my gift in his face.

He eyes us both suspiciously. "What's the password?"

"Um, Happy Birthday?" guesses Oscar.

An older man who looks like Ricky with a deep widow's peak comes up behind Ricky and lightly smacks the back of his head. "Welcome to Kiera's thirteenth birthday party, including a special preview of Trampoline Zone! My name is Mr. Kapoor, but you can just call me the Jumping King. You'll have to excuse my son, Ricky. I think all the jumping has jostled his brain." He opens the door wider and Ricky rolls his eyes, ducking under his dad's arm. "Shoes go in the wooden cubbies by the cash register, and presents go in the party room. Make sure to grab a fresh pair of socks! We've got a half hour of free-jumping time and then pizza, cake, and presents. After that there will be a full hour of jumping time, and we're even busting out the foam machine."

Our jaws drop in unison.

"Did you say a *foam* machine?" asks Oscar.

"Yes, sir. I don't kid around about fun." Mr. Kapoor leans forward. "We even have black lights."

My eyes go so huge they might just pop out of my head. Leave it to Kiera to have the coolest birthday party this town has ever seen.

As Oscar and I walk through the door, we're both frozen in awe. There are trampolines everywhere. Trampolines with basketball hoops and trampolines surrounding a giant foam pit and a rock-climbing wall and an obstacle course.

Loud, poppy music booms through the speakers. I'm pretty sure this is, like, the coolest place within a two-hundred-mile radius of Valentine, Texas. I almost want to turn to Mr. Kapoor and ask if this is some sort of mistake and if they meant to open this place in a bigger city, because up until now the best thing Valentine had going for it was the slide at the community pool, and last year it was closed for half the summer because part of the ladder had rusted out.

"Ho-ly cannoli," I finally utter.

"Um. Ditto," says Oscar wide-eyed. "Mega ditto."

After we put our shoes away and replace our regular socks with the neon-green Trampoline Zone socks, we take our gifts to the party room, where Mrs. Bryant is setting the table with emoji-themed plates and cups.

She looks up and clasps her hands together. "Oh, Sweet Pea! And Oscar too. Y'all get to jumpin'! Nate!" she calls, and then when no one answers, she shouts, "Nate!"

Mr. Bryant sticks his head in the door with the kind of expression I give my mom when she comes in my room without knocking. "What?" His face shifts a little when he sees me.

"Sweet Pea and Oscar are here," she says sweetly.

He nods curtly to the two of us, and another dad taps him on the shoulder, freezing for a minute as he sees me.

"Do you happen to know where Kiera is?" Mrs. Bryant asks.

"Uh, on a trampoline?"

Another mom walks through the door as Mr. Bryant turns to talk to the dads. "I think I saw her on the rock wall, Shawna."

Mrs. Bryant turns back to us. "You two oughta go find Kiera. She'll be thrilled to see you both."

Oscar and I file out of the room past Mr. Bryant and the other dads. Maybe it's all in my head, but there are hushed whispers as I walk by, and I swear I hear it—the word Dad used to explain why he couldn't stay with Mom and how it was no one's fault.

Gay.

Adults don't always act like they're supposed to. Besides Mrs. Young and her wife, there are only a few other gay people in town that I know of, so it shouldn't surprise me that people—even well-meaning ones—can't seem to talk about anything else.

What's it called? Gaydar or whatever? Yeah, my gaydar totally went off around that guy.

Liz really knows how to pick 'em, huh?

That's gonna screw that kid up real good.

By the looks of it, she's been eating her feelings.

I squeeze my eyes shut, and I nearly stuff my fingers in my ears. I'm not ashamed of Dad. (Or Oscar, for that matter!) These people don't know anything about me or Mom or Dad except for the things they whisper back and forth to each other in the produce section of Green's Grocers. And now look at 'em all. Making all sorts of assumptions and jumping to all kinds of conclusions.

Oscar turns to me and takes my hand. Can he hear them too? His face looks a little pained, and I can tell I'm not just making it up. Suddenly, I feel fiercely protective. It's not just Dad they're talking about. In a way, it's Oscar too. But whether or not Oscar is gay, it doesn't matter, because these people are just flat-out wrong.

I whisk him away from the wall of gossiping adults, stomping as much as any two seventh graders can wearing just socks on soft foam mats.

"Where to first?" he asks.

I swallow back the anger and anxiety swirling in my chest like a sandstorm. Neither of my parents have made their reason for getting divorced a secret, but something in me—the same thing that would jump in front of a moving car for Cheese—makes me want to stop anyone from saying anything mean or rude about Dad. To protect him.

"Sweet Pea?" asks Oscar. "Can we just go jump?"

My mom always says that sometimes the best thing you can do to show a bully that they're in the wrong is to live your very best life, and right now our very best life is jumping up and down until our heads spin. "Anywhere but the rock wall!" I finally say. "Just looking at that harness gives me a wedgie."

CHAPTER THIRTEEN

The Life of the Party

There are lines for almost everything at Trampoline Zone. I swear, Kiera invited the whole dang town. Except me, and even though I never expected to be invited, I can't help feeling a little hurt at the thought of how much trouble she went through to *not* invite me.

Oscar and I find one of the basic trampolines unoccupied, but it's still way better than any trampoline I've ever been on. There are even trampolines against the wall to bounce off. When I say kids are bouncing off the walls, I'm dead serious.

Jumping back and forth with Oscar is the most fun because we send each other higher and higher into the air. Being a bigger girl, it might make me feel a little self-conscious to do this with other people, but Oscar and I are around the same size. It's kind of like how it's no fun playing on a seesaw with friends who are way skinnier than you, because you just sit there on the ground opposite them like a sunken ship.

Like Oscar says, fat kids gotta stick together. The first time he said that, actually, I couldn't hide how much the thought of being called fat mortified me. But Oscar just shrugged and said, "Fat doesn't have to be a bad thing."

"Have you thought about what you're going to say when Kiera sees you?" he asks as we pass each other midair.

My mouth goes dry at the thought of it. "Happy birthday?"

Oscar bounces on his butt and I land beside him, and we both take a moment to sprawl out and catch our breath. "She's gonna be so mad," he says, whispering even though no one can hear us over the music.

I know Kiera's no angel, but I already feel kind of bad for crashing her birthday party and bringing her such a crummy present that she's going to have to open in front of everyone. But then I wonder if going to a party I was never even invited to will seem desperate and just make me look like an even bigger loser. It's like no matter how hard I try, the joke's always on me.

Oscar rolls over and props himself up on his side. "Are you okay? After, you know, what those parents were saying?"

I'm fine, but I can't help but wonder how that made Oscar feel. "Are you okay, though?"

He nods slowly. "I'm awesome."

"You really are, you know." I smile at him.

Greg bounces down onto our trampoline, sending us both flying into the air. "Incoming!" He laughs wildly. "Whoa, getting some serious air, Sweet Pea! Hey, I thought you said you weren't coming."

"Real smooth, pretty boy," Oscar mutters under his breath.

Suddenly I feel like the whole stinking Webster's dictionary is stuck in the pit of my stomach, and I can't think of a single word to say. "Uh-huh."

He jumps up and down again, but this time not as hard. "You wanna do the obstacle course together later?"

"Do I want to do obstacles with you?"

He jumps down again, and I bounce off my butt a few feet. "Uh, yeah. The obstacle course."

My cheeks are hotter than a house fire. How is it so warm in here? "Yeah, totally."

"It's a date then!" shouts Oscar.

I shoot poison eye daggers his way. Why would he ever say that?

Ricky jumps onto the trampoline behind us and blows his whistle. "Only two kids per trampoline in this zone." He points to a sign above our heads. "Read it and weep."

Greg flashes me two thumbs and then calls to Ricky over his shoulder. "Sorry, dude."

"I'm not your dude!" shouts Ricky.

"Whatever, dude," Greg shouts back. "I think he totally made that rule up," he says to me before he hops away.

I jump up in the air and land flat on my back, bursting out into a fit of giggles. "A date! Why would you even say that word?"

Oscar jumps up, throwing me a few feet in the air. "It's only a big deal if you make it a big deal, Sweet Pea." He lets out a *hmph* noise.

I tackle him and clap my hand over his mouth. "Don't tease me."

"I'm sorry, okay?" He stops bouncing and looks me in the eyes with total genuine concern.

I nod, because I know he means it. "It's okay."

"Attention, partygoers," says Ricky in a flat voice over the intercom. "Hip-hip hooray. It's time to celebrate Kiera's birthday."

"He sounds like a robot," Oscar snickers.

"Robot. Life. Confirmed," I respond in a computer voice.

Ricky's monotone voice crackles over the speaker again. "Head to the party room for pizza and cake. Presents too. Oh, joy."

Oscar claps his hands twice like a mechanical monkey. "This. Is. How. Robots. Party."

We laugh and continue our robot impressions as we shuffle into the party room behind a few other kids. Call it the curse of the fat girl or whatever you want, but Kiera can't miss me. Her eyes go wide, and her nostrils flare the moment she sees me. My cheeks turn red and I try to swallow, but my throat feels like sandpaper. Mrs. Bryant guides Oscar and me to a pair of seats opposite Kiera, and at the sight of her mother, she simmers.

Oscar settles in next to me and I do my best to make us invisible and let everyone else do the talking. Because Oscar is a good friend, he does that thing where he pretends like we're deep in conversation and exchanging jokes that only we get.

The whole party sings "Happy Birthday," and Kiera blows out the candles on the two-tier emoji cake she'd pouted about wanting during her class birthday party. I know Kiera said in her letter she wasn't a spoiled brat, but she's not really helping her image, if you ask me.

After cake is served, it's time to open presents. I almost forget about my gift until she holds my gift bag up to her ear and shakes it. Suddenly I want to sink into the floor. I should have just bought her lip gloss like Dad said. What was I thinking?

She reaches her hand in and comes up with the lint roller. "What even is this?"

"Oh," her mom says. "What a useful gift." She checks the tag on the bag. "From Sweet Pea." Her brow furrows a bit, but her voice stays just the same as she says, "How thoughtful."

Kiera reaches in once more and comes up with the deodorant. She lets out a disgusted scoff. "Um, are you trying to say something?"

Dread settles in my stomach. Like the time I thought painting Cheese's claws hot pink was a good idea.

I clear my throat. This is the moment when I should say something like, *Yeah, Kiera, your pits stink, and so does the way you ditched me in fourth grade.* But here in this room full of my classmates and their parents, all I can utter is, "I thought it smelled good."

Every kid in the room turns to me with various confused expressions. Even Greg. I thought I'd embarrass Kiera with my gift, but I didn't even think of all the ways this could backfire, and now I'm the one who looks like a total jerk who couldn't pick out a half-decent gift for a party she wasn't even invited to. Great.

Behind me, Mr. Bryant mutters, "DiMarco's kid *would* bring that gift."

Sometimes adults are mean. Tears prickle at the corners of my eyes, but I refuse to cry in the middle of Kiera's birthday party. Besides, I'm at least going to survive this long enough to make it to the foam-and-black-light part of the party.

Kiera glances at the puberty guidebook. "Wow, Sweet Pea." Her voice is flat and unimpressed. Then under her breath she says, "I'm pretty sure she needs this more than I do."

"What do you say, Kiera?" asks Mrs. Bryant.

"Thanks," she drawls. "I guess."

Oscar's knee knocks against mine. "That was hilarious," he says even though I can tell he doesn't totally mean it. "You really got her good."

Kiera opens the rest of her gifts, and she gets things like funny T-shirts, sparkly lip gloss, gift cards, and a few video games.

"All right!" says Mr. Kapoor. "Now that we've celebrated with cake, pizza, and presents, let's get to jumping!"

For a brief moment, my present debacle is forgotten as we race out to the basic trampolines. "How about we add some foam to this mix?" calls Mr. Kapoor over the speakers.

The whole party shrieks their approval.

The lights go out, and it's pitch black for a short second before we're all awash in black lights and everyone is glowing, especially anyone wearing lighter colors.

"Your teeth!" I shout to Oscar over the music. "They're glowing!"

"Yours are too!"

We clasp hands and jump up and down as pink and blue foam shoots out of a machine just off to the side of the trampolines. This is pretty awesome. Maybe crashing Kiera's birthday party and looking like a total dweeb was worth it.

Greg throws a handful of foam at my face, and I get him back, but he turns just in time so that it hits the back of his head.

I squeal as he lunges for more foam to launch at me and I'm having so much fun that I'm almost dizzy with it. Just then my stomach lurches and—*oh no*. It hits me. This isn't like the nerves I get when I have to talk in front of the whole class or the butterflies I've felt in my stomach every time I talk to Greg. It starts like a wave at the pit of my stomach, but then it turns into a volcano.

I don't feel so good.

My body doesn't even give me a second to try to hold it in.

I puke. Barf. Yak. Upchuck. Lose my lunch. Blow chunks. Whatever you want to call it. I vomit everywhere. And the first thing I can think is who in the heck had the genius idea to serve us cake and pizza before we jumped ourselves silly under black lights? Isn't this what adults are for? To predict all the ways something can go totally and completely awfully wrong? If I have to wait an hour after

I eat to swim, what adult in their right mind would pump me full of food and soda and then send me to bounce my face off in a trampoline park?

It takes a second for the people around me to notice that what they've just been sprayed with was definitely not foam.

I can feel the mortification setting in. I can already see how this moment will follow me for the rest of my life. All the way to high school graduation. I'll have to get far away from this town and everyone in it to escape this exact moment defining me in college and adulthood.

"Bring up the lights!" shouts Ricky.

It takes a minute for my eyes to adjust, but when they do, I see the damage, and it's not good. I guess it's not every day that you puke on your archnemesis, your BFF, a teenage boy, and a boy who makes you so nervous you feel like you could puke all over again.

I wrap my arms around my tummy. "I don't feel so good."

Oscar gasps. "Oh my gosh, Sweet Pea! Are you okay?" His voice drops a little when he realizes midsentence that he's also been targeted by the second coming of my pizza and cake.

Greg wipes a speck of my puke off his glasses. I wish I could magically disappear.

Kiera shrieks. "Did you really just puke on me? At my own birthday party? That you weren't even invited to, you weirdo! You've ruined it. You've ruined my whole party! This is so gross." Her eyes begin to water, and I can't believe she's the one who's about to cry when I just completely embarrassed myself in front of everyone.

"Kiera," Mrs. Bryant scolds. "Oh, Sweet Pea, let's call your parents. Or I mean, your mom. Or your dad."

Mr. Bryant grunts, and his wife swats at his arm, nailing him pretty hard.

She looks back to me. "Who should we call, dear?"

My gaze scans the room, and I see the face of every single person in my class. They're an even split between horror and hysterical laughter. "My dad," I say, my lip quivering as I begin to cry. I can't hold it in this time.

My mouth tastes sour, and I feel a little sweaty and dizzy, but no amount of discomfort can quiet the fiery rage I feel.

It's official. I hate Kiera Bryant.

Dear Miss Flora Mae,

This is the second time I'm writing to you, even though you never responded to my first letter. I'm not sure if my letter got lost or what, but I'm trying again. I think my best friend is dumping me. She's hanging out with new girls who are older than me. And even though I think this is not at all important when deciding to be friends with someone, they're prettier and skinnier than me too. She's been avoiding me all summer, and I'm scared I'm going to start fifth grade best friend-less.

Sometimes I get really angry and I wonder if it's even worth trying to win her back. What's the point?

But she's my first real best friend, and I can't imagine my heart ever hurting more than it does right now. I want her to be my best friend again, but do I even want to be friends with someone who would dump me so easily?

Sincerely,
Heartbroken in Valentine

CHAPTER FOURTEEN

Ask and You Shall Receive

Dad picks me up from Trampoline Zone almost immediately. Thankfully he was nearby since the party was almost over, anyway.

He's not so good at taking care of me when I'm sick. Not because he's a bad dad, but because Mom always did that. It's like Dad took care of me when I was in a bad mood or had a bad idea and Mom was always there for all the times when I was sick and needed real taking care of.

He does his best, though, tucking me into bed and leaving a big glass of water on the nightstand. It's not dark yet, but he shuts all my blinds and sets up his laptop so I can watch whatever I want.

As I'm lying there, I hear Dad let Mom in the front

door. I turn down the volume on my show to hear what they're saying.

"Where is she?" my mom asks in a rush.

"She's lying down. She's fine, Liz."

"I can take her for the night. I don't mind."

"Let me do this," says Dad firmly but nicely.

Mom pauses for a moment. "In front of the whole party? She threw up in front of everyone?"

"More like she threw up *on* everyone. Poor kid."

"What was she even doing at Kiera's party in the first place?" She doesn't bother hiding the blame in her voice. "You knew they'd grown apart. And honestly, after the way Nate treated you when you told him about the divorce and . . . you . . . Andre, honestly, it's no better than sending her into the lion's den."

"I don't know, Liz. It's not Kiera's fault that her father's a homophobe. And I thought maybe she and Sweet Pea had made up. Stranger things have happened." He pauses for a moment. "They don't really cover this in all your parenting books, you know. There's no chapter on 'I've just told my daughter I'm gay and am attempting to navigate her social food chain while maintaining my own sanity.'"

For a moment, there's nothing but silence. And it's hard for me not to imagine Mom reaching over and taking Dad's hand. I know everything has changed for them, but how do you just turn it off? How do you just stop loving someone? Mom and Dad weren't just Mom and Dad. They were best friends too.

My doorknob moves, and I freeze, making the split-second decision to close my eyes and pretend to be asleep. Sometimes it's just easier to pretend.

I can't see her, but I can sense my mother's presence as she walks across my bedroom. I wonder how this house feels to her. I wish I could see it through her eyes. Does she see all the ways it's a sad dupe for our real home?

She leans over me and closes the laptop before pressing her lips to my forehead. "I'll see you tomorrow, baby."

When the door closes again, I open my eyes to find it totally dark. The sun has set, and without the light of the laptop, it's just me and the intensely embarrassing memory of this afternoon. I wish Cheese was here.

"Hey, uh, Liz," my dad says on the other side of the door. "I've been waiting on some important mail. Those documents from the bank in Connecticut. You haven't seen anything come through with my name on it, have you?"

"I sent Sweet Pea over with a few things that came in, but that's all I've seen."

"Huh. That's weird. I'll check with her."

Connecticut? Grandma lives in Connecticut, and it's clear across the country. I've visited a few times, but mostly she just comes to see us to get away from the cold winters. Why would Dad be waiting on papers from a bank in Connecticut?

Panic balloons in my chest, and even though there's not a thing left in my stomach, I think I might just puke all over again.

When I flip over on my side and pull my pillow tight to my cheek, my fingers slide against a piece of paper. Kiera's letter. I'd almost forgotten.

My panic dissolves into rage.

Kiera wants an answer to all her problems? Fine. I'll give her an answer.

Quietly I make my way to my desk and use my mini flashlight to find a piece of paper and a pencil.

Dear Not a Spoiled Brat, I write, but I press so hard the tip of my pencil snaps.

I take a deep breath. This is for all the times I wasn't quick enough on my feet to think of a comeback and for all the times Kiera's made me look like a fool and for completely cutting me out of her life when I wasn't cool enough anymore. I dig out a new pencil and try again.

Dear Not a Spoiled Brat,
I think you're suffering from a medical condition known as the me-me-mes. Sometimes the best advice is the toughest to hear, but it sounds like you need a whole bunch of the tough stuff. Have you ever

considered that maybe right now you are the least of your parents' worries? You say you're not a spoiled brat, but what if you're the reason your parents can't stand each other? I wouldn't be surprised if a lot of their disagreements start with you. You want to know what? Sometimes adults are too easy on kids. Everyone always tells kids it's not their fault, but maybe it is. Maybe it's time to grow up and be a little more thankful for all the things you have. Maybe Not a Spoiled Brat is 100 percent a spoiled brat after all.

Sincerely,
Miss Flora Mae

Ask and you shall receive, Kiera Bryant.

CHAPTER FIFTEEN

R-E-S-P-E-C-T

The next morning, Dad doesn't even bother waking me up on time for school, and after having a stream of nightmares where I opened jack-in-the-box after jack-in-the-box with Kiera's head popping out instead of a clown's, I'm happy to spend a day at home. I ruined my perfect attendance record back when my parents announced their divorce anyway. I locked myself in my room and went on a hunger strike. (Though to be fair, my parents were totally unaware of the emergency Doritos I stole from the kitchen on day two.)

Miss Flora Mae said Joe would be picking up her letters on Monday afternoon, so once Dad has run out to give someone a quote on a paint job and I'm sure my mom has left for the office, I head over to Miss Flora Mae's.

During the day, this place is still totally weird, but a whole lot less creepy than it was at night. The 100-percent-dead cat is still sitting there on the mantel, and I decide, *Heck! If you can't beat 'em, join 'em.* "Hey, Bette Davis," I say to the cat. "You haven't moved an inch since the last time I saw you."

Now, if she had, that would be something to completely freak out about.

I head back to the sunroom where Miss Flora Mae keeps most of her plants and find a stereo so old it's bigger than the giant printer in the attendance office. Taped to the side is a faded piece of paper with a few favorite radio stations penned in Miss Flora Mae's handwriting. I turn the thing on and am hit with a wall of static.

"Yowza!" I screech and clap my hands over my ears.

I flip through the channels until I land on 109.8 Soul Food. The station is on a commercial right now for a cell phone repair shop, but I pipe up the volume so even the plants on the screened-in front porch can hear.

After grabbing a can of ginger ale from the fridge, I walk around to the little door that leads out to the porch and sit down at Miss Flora Mae's desk in front of her pea-green typewriter. I open the drawer and find an old pair of bright-red cat-eye glasses with the lenses missing. I examine them for a minute before putting them on. Feels right.

Over the speakers, a man with a deep, smooth voice says, "Welcome back, my lunchtime angels. Let's settle into this noon hour with a classic from the queen herself, Miss Aretha Franklin. This one's dedicated to all you out there workin' for the man. R-E-S-P-E-C-T, baby."

And then I begin to type. The music sinks into my bones, and the song sounds a little familiar, like I might have heard it in a movie or something. But this Miss Aretha lady feels every word she sings. She feels it so hard that I do too. I get why Miss Flora Mae calls her the queen. Her voice makes me feel like I've got fire in my toes, spreading all the way up to my chest.

Typing my handwritten letter to Kiera so that it looks like it came straight from Miss Flora Mae takes a little while. I think I've heard about six or seven songs before I'm done. I definitely hit the wrong keys more than twice and have to start over, because there's no backspace button on this dinosaur. Reloading the paper is a little tricky, but eventually I get it right.

When I'm done, I check on the plants once more and turn the radio off, even though I actually think I could sit here for a while longer, just listening, especially to Miss Aretha Franklin.

After locking up the house and leaving the cat-eye glasses where I found them, I add the reply letter and Kiera's original letter to the package of letters that will go to print this week.

R-E-S-P-E-C-T, baby. R-E-S-P-E-C-T.

CHAPTER SIXTEEN

Neutral Territory

If I could brush all my hair in front of my face and just go to school as a giant head of hair instead of as Sweet Pea the Projectile Puker, I would, but the fact is I wouldn't be able to see where I'm going.

Mom insists on driving me to school and I don't fight her, because I'm more than happy to not face the bus crowd today. About a block away from school, Mom pulls over onto a neighborhood street.

"What's wrong?" I ask. It feels like she's about to say something heavy and serious, but it's not like she's getting another divorce.

She gives me a soft smile. "Nothing's wrong, Sweet Pea.

I just wanted to be sure that you understand you have nothing to be embarrassed about."

I want so badly to plug my fingers in my ears and scream *la, la, la, la, la!*

Reaching over the parking brake, she pats my thigh. "Sometimes bodies are just bodies—"

"And what?" I ask. "Are you going to tell me it's perfectly natural to puke all over my classmates?"

"No," she says, her thinning patience showing. "I was going to say that sometimes bodies are just bodies and there's not much we can do about it."

I wedge myself against the door, trying to push down the little prickles of guilt I feel for not just letting her be nice and comfort me. "But did my body have to be such a *body* in front of my whole class?"

Her shoulders shake as she chuckles. "Chalk that up to a mystery of the universe, my dear. It's like that gosh darn news cycle," she says. "Someone will come along and do something even more memorable and no one will ever remember about your incident, so you hold your head up high, baby."

I roll my eyes, but really she makes me feel a little bit better.

She pulls back out into the street. "If you'd rather," she says, "we can talk about the research project you've got coming up. I haven't seen you do even a little bit of work on it, you know."

I groan. I've got no clue what I'm going to do for that project, and if I don't get my act together soon, I might not even make it to eighth grade. "Can we go back to talking about me puking on my whole class?"

At school, I don't exactly hold my head up high, but at least I don't hide under my desk.

The moment I step out of Mom's car, Oscar is on me like a magnet. At first, he doesn't ask questions or prod. He called to check up on me while I was home from school, but no official word on the *incident.*

"Pretending it didn't happen makes it worse," I blurt.

He lets out a big sigh. "I just . . . I didn't even know what to say when it happened, and I feel like I should have said something or done something more than—"

"Well, to be fair, you *were* covered in puke."

He gives me a half smile. "Honestly, my brothers have covered me in grosser things."

"That's comforting," I say. "Today is going to be the worst. I already know it."

He holds an arm out in front of me like Mom does when she slams on the brakes. "Your human shield! I solemnly swear to be your human shield."

And he really follows through.

There are a few snickers, and a couple of boys make gagging noises as I walk past them, but other than that and Kiera holding her nose as I walk to my desk, the school day is off to an okay start. During lunch, even Greg avoids making eye contact with me.

In the afternoon, there's a knock on our door, and Miss Horton pokes her head in. "Kiera Bryant? I've got a message for you from your mother."

A few students, Oscar included, let out a dramatic *ooooooooo*.

Kiera tucks her hair behind her ears and takes the note from Miss Horton. After taking a moment to read it, she says, "Mrs. Young, may I be excused to the restroom?" Her voice is lacking that normal bounce I've come to be so annoyed by.

Mrs. Young doesn't even look up from her lesson plan. "Be sure to take the girls' bathroom pass and be quick about it."

Kiera stands, and her long braids swing forward so I can't see her face. She takes the girls' pass, a laminated golden ticket, from the hook by the door.

We have ten minutes of free reading left, and I do my best to concentrate on *A Wrinkle in Time*, but then it hits me.

I have to pee.

I try to remember all the mental tricks my dad has

ever tried to teach me during a road trip, but every time I close my eyes all I see is running water. Faucets. Streams. Waterfalls. Waves. If it's got water, it's stuck in my head. Pools. Hot tubs.

No, come on, Sweet Pea. Hold it.

Deserts. Sand dunes. Sandy deserts. Desert oasis.

Nope. I gotta go. Now.

Mrs. Young is so strict with her bathroom passes. She wasn't always this way, but when Trevor Watkins got caught lighting one of his dad's cigars in the boys' bathroom last December, every teacher cracked down on bathroom passes.

My hand shoots up in the air. I might be Sweet Pea the Puker, but I'm not about to become Sweet *Pee* the Puker.

Mrs. Young doesn't see me, and I begin to squirm in my seat and wave my hand in the air, like I'm drowning in the deep end. I smack my forehead with my free hand. Oh great. Another water reference.

"Yes, Sweet Pea?" she finally says.

"I've got to go to the restroom," I say. "Pronto."

"You can go the moment Miss Bryant returns."

"But ma'am—"

"Mrs. Young," says Joseph "Digging for Gold" Russo, biting back laughter. "If Sweet Pea says it's an emergency, you might want to trust her on that." And then under his breath he adds, "I've got the puke-stained T-shirt from this weekend to prove it."

I want to snap right back with an equal amount of snark, but his plea works.

"All right," she says. "Take the boys' pass and please bring Miss Bryant back with you. No detours."

I pop up and take the other pass. "Yes, ma'am!"

I speed walk to the restroom at the end of the hallway and let out an actual sigh of relief the moment my tush hits the porcelain toilet seat.

It's not until I'm washing my hands that I hear the sniffling from the handicap stall and remember what Mrs. Young said about bringing Kiera back with me.

"Hello?" I call out as I dry my hands on the front of my shirt. "Kiera?"

"What do you want?" Her voice sounds like a live wire.

"How do you even know who it is?" I ask.

"Oh, I'd know *that* voice anywhere. If I were dead, I'd still hear your voice and know it was you haunting me in my grave, Sweet Pea."

I heave out a sigh. "Well, you can't say I'm not memorable."

I try to muster all the fiery anger I've felt for Kiera over the last few days, but hearing the way her voice quivers makes it hard to be mean. Almost like it's no fun if she can't fight back. "You wanna tell me what's up?"

"Not really." The stall door swings open and she stomps

out. I didn't know girls like Kiera could stomp. I figured she glided or floated everywhere.

"You probably don't remember, but I'm a pretty good listener."

"I remember you listening," she says. "It's the judging I don't like."

I try to hide the shock registering on my face. I'm not judgmental. How could she ever say that?

"Okay, fine." She heaves a sigh. "It's my parents. They're the worst."

"Your parents aren't bad," I tell her. At least half of them aren't.

"You try living with them when they can't even say good morning without my dad yelling or my mom crying." She crumples up the note from the office and tosses it in the trash can. "And now my mom says I have to take the bus home today."

"You—you're crying because you have to take the bus home today?"

I always knew Kiera's family had way more money than mine and that her life was what Mom always called "charmed," but lately the only way I've gotten out of taking the bus was by puking all over my whole seventh-grade class.

She lets out a deep groan. "It's not the stinking bus.

It's like—doesn't it ever feel like all the stuff in your life is building up, and then it just takes the silliest thing for it to all come toppling over and you just, like, lose it over that one ridiculous thing?"

It's like the wind's been knocked out of me because I know that feeling so, so well, and never in all my life did I think Kiera and I would ever find anything in common again. "Yeah, actually. I know exactly what that feels like."

She reaches past me for the soap dispenser and starts to wash her hands.

"So your parents aren't getting along?" I ask.

"That's putting it mildly." She dries her hands and shoulders past me.

Something inside me is desperate to keep her in this bathroom so I can hear more. Maybe it was the letter she sent. Or maybe a small part of me thinks we have more common ground than I thought. "No one gets it," I finally say. "It's like your parents being married is one of those things that's supposed to last forever. No one gets what it's like when that just ends out of nowhere."

"It's like finding out the tooth fairy isn't real." Kiera turns around, and her face looks like I've sucked every bit of air out of her. "It's all I can think about. Sometimes I just ask for stuff I don't need or throw fits over silly things so that they can argue over that stuff instead. That at least feels normal."

I shake my head, remembering how I lied to my dad about his mail. I don't even know what I was trying to do. Just get some kind of reaction out of the two of them, I guess. Because right now in their weird perfect little divorce world with their perfect little houses on the same street, I feel like a broken compass just spinning in circles, trying to find my way. Like, I'm just looking for a sign—any kind of sign—that will tell me how I'm supposed to feel.

I take a step closer to her. "I'm sorry for crashing your party and for giving you that dumb gift."

She shrugs. "The deodorant actually did smell good."

"And for puking on you."

"That was, like, the grossest thing ever," she says, but then as though she's just realized we're not being jerks to each other right now, she adds, "but maybe it wasn't such a great idea to hit the trampolines after all that pizza and cake."

"It was still a pretty cool party."

She pauses for a moment. "We better get back to class."

I hate to leave the bathroom, where it felt like we were in neutral territory for a little while, a place where neither of us had to worry about what had happened in the past, but I'd also hate to get in trouble for taking too long in the restroom. The two of us take our hall passes and walk back to Mrs. Young's room in silence.

It feels like something between us has shifted. But I

still can't forget what the last three years have been like and what it felt like to be ditched by the person I trusted most.

Guilt settles in my stomach as I think about the letter I wrote Kiera. Not even my worst enemy deserves a letter like that.

After school, Mrs. Young must see the worry on my face, because when everyone is getting their stuff together to walk out to the pickup lines, she says, "Sweet Pea, hang back for a minute if you don't mind."

Oscar looks over at me, and I just shrug. "I'll meet you outside."

Once the room has cleared, Mrs. Young sits down at the desk beside me, tucking her black dress with multicolored beetles underneath her. Today she wears a light-pink lipstick, with her hair twisted into a sloppy bun and secured with two paintbrushes.

"How's it going?" she asks, like it's not at all weird that she asked me to stay after school.

"Am I in trouble?" I ask. "Is this about my research project?"

She shakes her head. "You're not in trouble, but you do need to let me know who your project is on and soon. That's not why I asked you to stay, though. I just wanted to check in with you. I know we talked a few months ago, but you seemed a little off today."

Mrs. Young was one of the first people to know that Mom and Dad were getting a divorce. They told her because they wanted her to know what was going on in case I wasn't myself.

"I'm okay."

"Everything okay at home?"

I nod. "Yeah."

"You know," she says, "you've got a lot of big changes going on right now. It's okay if you need to readjust a little bit. No one expects you to just act like everything is fine."

"Thanks," I say, trying to release the knot of tension gathered in my forehead.

"But that's not all that's bothering you today, is it?" she asks.

I shake my head.

"Anything I can help with?"

I take a breath. "I think I've made a big mistake, and I don't know what I'm going to do."

"You know, the best part about mistakes is there's nowhere to go but up. You can either learn from them or if you're really lucky, you might even be able to fix them."

"Too bad life isn't written in pencil," I say.

She laughs at that. "That'd be a seriously giant number-two pencil."

CHAPTER SEVENTEEN

A Girl on a Mission

I speed walk to the bus and pray for it to drive as fast as it can so I can get home. Life might not be written in pencil, but maybe Mrs. Young is right. Maybe some mistakes can be fixed.

The minute the bus hits my stop, I'm running out the door and down the street.

Oscar, who is supposed to be hanging out at my house after school, jogs behind me. "Hey! Wait for me! You still haven't told me why Mrs. Young made you stay after school!"

Panting, I open the mailbox. The letters. They're all gone.

"Sweet Pea, that's not even your mailbox," he says as he catches up to me.

I turn to him, my hand on my chest. I haven't told him a peep about my little job for Miss Flora Mae. She told me not to tell anyone, and I haven't. But Oscar's my best friend.

Except that doesn't matter right now. All that matters is that I wrote a totally horrendous letter to Kiera, and for all I know, it's already gone to print for the Thursday paper. The *Valentine Gazette* runs on Tuesdays, Thursdays, and Sundays. There's just not enough news here for seven days' worth of newspapers.

"Oscar. Oh my gosh, please don't hate me. But I can't hang out today."

His whole face drops. "But I took your bus home."

"I know. I'm so, so sorry." I feel so guilty, but I've got to fix this, and I have to do it alone.

"Are you mad at me or something?"

I wave my hands up like I'm trying to erase something from a chalkboard. "Heck no. No, I just have something I gotta do that I totally forgot about."

"Something I can't do with you?"

I hold my breath for a moment. "I'm sorry. I promise I'll make it up to you."

He shrugs. "Fine. I guess I'll walk home."

"I really am sorry."

"Whatever," he says, and turns to start the walk to his house.

"Friday night!" I yell. "Sleepover at my dad's."

He doesn't turn around. "Yeah. Sure."

I feel awful, but I'm too panicked to let it fester. I race into my mom's house and drop my things before running back over to Miss Flora Mae's.

"What's up, Bette Davis?" I wave to the still very dead cat without missing a beat before letting myself into the screened-in porch and settling in.

I sit there for a moment, totally unsure of what to write. Something's not right.

I run back to the sunroom and turn on the stereo, but none of the radio stations are playing what I'm looking for. I sit down on the floor and begin digging through a crate of old records and CDs. I don't actually know how to use Miss Flora Mae's record player, but I figure her CD player can't be any different than Dad's DVD player, so I flip through until I find a cracked CD case that says *Greatest Hits*, and I slip it into the CD player, praying it works.

It takes a moment before a piano begins to play and Miss Aretha's voice sings, "You better think. Think about what you're trying to do to me . . ."

That's the stuff. I crank the volume up and settle in behind Miss Flora Mae's desk on the front screened-in porch.

I open the drawers for a second, just nosing around, and stumble upon the cat-eye glasses without the lenses. I put them on and close my eyes, thinking about what I would need to hear if I were in Kiera's shoes. *You better think.*

And then I begin to type.

Once I've got my letter all set, I dig my bike out of the garage. It's been a hot minute since I used this thing because the chain on Oscar's bike broke last year and he hasn't gotten a new one yet, so we walk just about everywhere our parents won't drive us. Valentine is easy enough to get around. The downtown is just one single square where the newspaper, city hall, and a few other random shops, like Bill's Boots & Cobbler, By Design Florals, and The Jerky Emporium, which sells nothing but—you guessed it—jerky, all surround a bronze Cupid statue next to a big sign that says "Welcome to Valentine, the Heart of Texas." Mom says the Cupid statue was bought by some rich oil investor as kind of a joke, but that the town takes it very seriously.

To get to downtown, I have to cross six blocks and Ancestors' Park, which was the town's first graveyard, but so much of it was destroyed during a tornado that it's hard to tell where it starts and ends. Honestly, Valentine should be on *America's Most Haunted*, if you ask me. Cliff Van-Warren would find plenty of stories to tell in this place.

As I pedal down my driveway to embark on my journey, the tassels on my handlebars feel childish, and I can't believe I ever even wore this helmet with a unicorn horn sticking out the front, but I did, and now I am again.

"Let's ride," I say to myself as I take a wide turn out of my driveway and pedal toward downtown.

Passing the park, I stand up on my pedals and move as fast as I can. "Not haunted, not haunted, not haunted, not haunted, not haunted." Above me a bird squawks. "A little haunted, a little haunted, a little haunted, a little haunted."

The paper is located just off the main square, in between the civic center and the library. I hadn't really thought about how I might get in, especially since the place is already closed. This is ridiculous. What was I even thinking? Maybe this is like Mrs. Young said and this is the kind of mistake I'll have to learn from instead of fix.

I turn my bike around, but as I do, I spot a light spilling out into the alleyway. Walking my bike down the alleyway, I find a side door left open. Maybe there's hope yet! After ditching my bike behind the dumpster, I duck my head inside to find the janitor, a tall, bearded guy who looks a whole heck of a lot like Hagrid from Harry Potter. If I weren't here on a mission, I might ask him to say *You're a wizard, Sweet Pea!* to me.

Heavy metal music crackles through his earphones as

he deep lunges like he's rocking out live in concert while he slides the vacuum across the floor. With his back turned to me, I tiptoe around him. When he moves in one direction, I do the opposite.

I pay close attention to vacuuming Hagrid and try to check all the names on the office doors. *Senior Copy Editor: Carol Tinsley, Lead Photographer: Sam Ortega, Sports Editor: Zoe Corbin* . . .

I gasp! *Editor in Chief: Joe Salazar.* I turn for his office and stub my toe right on the corner of a cubicle. The wall of the cubicle rocks back and forth, and I catch it with one hand, while hopping on one foot and trying so hard not to scream my head off. Yowza!

When the throbbing in my big toe subsides, I check the handle on Mr. Joe's door. Unlocked! Looking back and forth and with eyes on Hagrid, I let myself into the office and close the door behind me.

I take a moment to let out a long-held breath. Mr. Joe's office is covered in framed articles and a few certificates and diplomas. His desk is littered with coffee cups and food-stained papers. This place is a mess, and I don't know which way is up. What the heck am I even doing? I don't know how newspapers work or where Miss Flora Mae's letters might be. And with that giant dude out there cleaning, I'm like a sitting duck!

Okay, okay, okay. Be cool, Sweet Pea. I start checking drawers and cabinets and thumbing through papers. This guy has enough paper in his office to make up a whole forest. Geez.

I hear the knob on the door turn. Oh dang!

I hide in the only place I can, under Mr. Joe's desk next to his trash can, which definitely contains an old bologna sandwich or two. Footsteps clomp around the desk until two very giant work boots stand before me.

I clap my hand over my mouth as the janitor reaches under the desk. I press my body against the back of the desk, doing my best to make myself small, which, to be honest, is not an easy task for me.

His hand continues to search until—the trash can! He's looking for the trash can. Despite the heavy metal music still blaring from his headphones, I do my best not to make any noise as I slide the metal bin into his grasp.

He pulls the trash can and I hold my breath as he changes the bags before tossing the trash can back under the desk and completely nailing me in the shin. I can't contain the yelp that slips from my mouth.

The big work boots don't move.

He heard me. He so totally heard me.

The music grows louder as he tugs his earbuds out of his ears and stands perfectly still for a moment.

Hagrid lets out a loud *hmmph* before walking back out of the office and slamming the door.

I collapse onto the floor, and holy cannoli, that was a close one. My nerves are shot. I was not meant for a life of crime, that's for dang sure.

And then I see it. Sitting on top of the filing cabinet behind Mr. Joe's desk, Miss Flora Mae's envelope sits, unopened.

Carefully, I open the envelope and swap the letters out, doing my best to reseal it while also crossing my fingers that Mr. Joe isn't sensitive to details. Based on the state of his office, though, I think I might've lucked out.

I crack the office door and wait for the janitor to walk into one of the other offices before I make a run for the back door. My bike is right where I left it, and by an act of God or maybe just a late client, I beat my mom home from work with just enough time to pretend I'm knee-deep in homework. Maybe there are some benefits to only having one set of parental eyes on you at a time.

My brain is running a thousand miles a minute. I wonder what Kiera will think when she sees her letter and my response in the paper. I hope Oscar isn't still mad at me. And what the heck was Dad even talking about when he mentioned papers from a bank in Connecticut to Mom?

Cheese rolls around on my math homework and leaves

a loving bite mark on the top corner of my grammar worksheet. Who can even think about long division or participles at a time like this? I glance down at the date on my calendar and count out the days. I have less than thirteen actual school days before I'm officially an eighth grader. How did I go from hanging out with Oscar bored out of our minds just last week to my life completely exploding all at once?

I scratch the top of Cheese's head as he nudges my history book off the kitchen table and rolls over on his side so that he looks like a crescent roll–shaped cat. "You're not being very helpful, but I appreciate the thought."

Mom walks in from work a few minutes later, tired circles under her eyes, and finds me at the kitchen table, trying to do homework. She plops down beside me and Cheese hops into her lap. After taking a look at me, she says, "Looks like we both had long days, huh?"

I shut my history book with a loud thud. "You're not kidding."

"School okay?" she asks. "No one gave you a hard time about getting sick at the party, did they?"

"Nah, it was fine."

She reaches over and pushes my bangs out of my face a little. "You want to ditch dinner at home and see a movie?"

"Are you serious?" Mom isn't usually the type of

parent to spring a trip to the movies on a school night, but whatever's gotten into her is working in my favor.

"Serious as my love for buttered popcorn."

Mom loops her foot around the leg of my chair and drags me closer to her, slinging an arm over my shoulder and giving me a quick kiss on the forehead.

CHAPTER EIGHTEEN

Paper, Paper, Get Your Paper!

"Sweet Pea," my mom coos in my ear.

I lie curled on my side with Cheese purring into my chest. "Noooo," I moan. "Just ten more minutes."

Mom squeezes into my twin bed, making a Cheese sandwich. He lets out a low yowl and repositions himself on top of my feet.

"How is it already Thursday?" Mom asks. "At least I get Thursday this week."

I almost say something sarcastic about how maybe we wouldn't have to split my days between the both of them if they'd just figured out a way to stay together. But I don't say anything because for Mom, the divorce was some kind of major failure. Like, not only were things messed up between her and Dad, but what kind of therapist can't even keep her own family together? I think that's where her mirror-house theory came from. If she was going to fail, at least she could be really good at it.

The day Mom and Dad sat me down to tell me they were getting a divorce, I knew immediately something was up. They waited until after Christmas, and the thought of that—them deciding to give me one last Christmas with us all together—makes me feel a little lucky and a little sad at the same time. It was a Sunday morning in January, and I woke up to the smell of cinnamon rolls. The homemade kind. Mom and Dad always made breakfast, but never something like this that was basically all dessert.

They let me finish one whole cinnamon roll before Mom said, "Sweet Pea, we have something to tell you." I froze and looked up at them.

Dad took Mom's hand. Mom always had to do the serious stuff, so I remember thinking it was so weird that Dad was the one to drop the news. "You know your mother and I love each other very much. We love you most of all. But Mom and I have decided not to live together anymore, which is why we're getting a divor—"

Mom coughed loudly, the kind of cough that sounded fake.

Dad gave her a look and then tried again. "Your mother and I have decided to end our marriage."

I guess for whatever reason my mom had some issue with the *D* word. It took me a minute to get what he was saying, but then all at once his words sank in, and all I felt was the hollowness of shock in my chest. This was the last thing I'd expected. I had even thought maybe Mom was pregnant or that we were moving. Mom had always talked about teaching at a university. But this? Mom and Dad getting a divorce? I couldn't believe it.

Nothing about it made sense. They were happy. We were happy. "W-w-why?" I asked, brimming with tears. "What happened?"

Mom looked to Dad, like that was his cue.

He reached across the table and took my hand, sticky from cinnamon roll icing, so that he was holding mine and Mom's hands. "Sweet Pea, I need to tell you something. It's something I think I've known for quite a long time, but I thought maybe it would go away."

Tears began to roll down my cheeks. "Are you sick?" I turned to Mom. "Is Dad dying?"

"Oh, mercy, no," she said, almost laughing, but not in a cheerful way.

Dad squeezed my hand and gave me a hopeless-looking smile. "I'm not sick. There's nothing wrong with me. But Sweet Pea, I'm gay."

I sat there for a while, the only thing finally breaking the silence was Cheese jumping on the counter to lick a spatula. Besides Mrs. Young and her wife, most of the gay people I knew of were on TV. Mom and Dad had always made sure I knew there was nothing wrong about being gay, and they'd even made a point of making me watch all the celebrations on the news when gay marriage was legalized. Mom said it was history being made. And I think one of Dad's cousins is gay. But other than that and the possibility of Oscar being gay, I hadn't thought about it very much.

In the end, though, Dad being gay was the kind of information I filed away in my brain to deal with some other time, because the real, looming issue I couldn't stop thinking about was the fact that my family was suddenly falling apart.

"Why can't you just stay with us?" I found myself asking. "It doesn't have to be a big deal." I knew they couldn't stay together. I knew it even then, but I had to ask.

Dad cleared his throat like that might somehow stop the tears rolling down his cheeks.

"We wish things could be the same, Sweet Pea," Mom said, her voice cracking on my name. "And we'll do our best to make sure things stay as close to the same for you as possible. We promise you. Right, Andre?"

Dad nodded firmly. "As little change as possible."

"Then why can't you just stay?" I asked again, but this time it came out more like a wail.

"I wish it could be that simple," Dad said with a sigh. "But that's not really fair to your mom. Or me."

"We still love each other very much," Mom said, her tears finally spilling over. "We'll always be best friends, but more than that, we'll always be your parents. Just as we always have been."

And maybe that's when it all started—this idea of two nearly identical houses and their promise to keep things as normal as possible. Mom and Dad talked for a while, and some of it I heard while some of it just felt like a ringing noise in my ears. Sometimes when I remember it all, I still feel the sting like it's a fresh wound.

It's easiest to forget they're even divorced at all in the morning, like now, when I'm still curled up in bed and half-asleep. But then, like sunlight burning against my eyelids, I remember that no matter how hard Mom and Dad try, things will never be the same. I let out a long yawn and cling to Mom's side like a koala as a last-ditch effort to keep her in bed.

"No fair," she says and stands up. Her phone vibrates in her pocket and she takes it out to look at her message. She grins from ear to ear and lets out a giggle.

"What is it?" I ask.

"Oh," she says, caught off guard, and puts her phone away. "Just a funny text from your aunt."

I groan, not yet able to shake myself free of sleepiness. "Come on. Lay down with me for just five more minutes."

"I see what you're doing," Mom says. "You're trying to tempt me with cuddles. Come on. Let's move it. Just two more days until the weekend!"

Ahhh, the weekend. I can't wait. But first I have to survive Thursday. *Wait, Thursday! Holy cannoli!* Suddenly I'm wide awake. The paper is running today!

I shoot up quick and scare Cheese off the bed. Without even a speck of grace, I stumble out of bed and race to the front door, where the paper is waiting.

This is it. What if I was totally wrong and they'd already sent the first letter to print? What if I messed up somehow and Mr. Joe knows I'm not Miss Flora Mae?

Only one way to find out.

I tear the plastic off the paper and open it up to the middle crease where the top of the page reads *MISS FLORA MAE I?*

"Whoa there," says Mom from over my shoulder. "When did you develop such an interest in current events?"

I shrug and hold the paper to my chest. "Just a fan of our lovely neighbor's advice column."

"Hmmm. You know, I wasn't always one myself, but

I guess I'm starting to turn a corner. Must have been all those mornings hearing your father read her letters at the kitchen table."

"I'm gonna get ready for school," I say and slip past her into the bathroom.

"Did you just take the newspaper into the bathroom?" she asks through the door.

I sit down on the edge of the tub. "Maybe?"

"You're too young to be a middle-aged man," she calls out as the sound of footsteps heads toward the kitchen.

I hold the paper out and search for my letter.

"Oh. My. Word." There I am at the bottom of the page. I mean, Miss Flora Mae, technically.

Dear Not a Spoiled Brat,

No matter which way you slice it, there's nothing easy about watching your parents fight. No one knows how hard it is when the two people you count on most can't deliver. But I guess parents are people too.

It's probably easy to look at what's happening and think that surely you could have prevented it. But that's just about as useful as an umbrella in a hurricane. I can't tell you what's going to happen next

and if your parents will weather this
storm. Maybe they'll make it and maybe
they won't.

Sometimes the hardest thing in the world
is figuring out that you're not in control.

Sincerely,

Miss Flora Mae

I know that I wrote the darn thing myself, so it feels
a little silly to think this, but something about this letter makes even me feel better. It's hard for me to piece
together my feelings about Kiera, but if anything, I know
what she's going through, so I hope this letter helps her
just a little.

Cheese's paw reaches under the door, yanking on it.
"Yeah, yeah, yeah," I say. "I'm almost done."

Oscar isn't waiting for me on the bus like he usually is, so
I just head right into Mrs. Young's class. He was out sick
yesterday, and I forgot to call him. If he's out again today, I
might just have to make a house call.

But when I walk into class, there he is at his desk,
flocked by Alyssa, Samantha, and Tyler, his friends from
the Valentine Community Theater's production of *The
Best Christmas Pageant Ever.*

Those friend thieves! I knew it!

Oscar's eyes flash on me for a second, but then he turns back to his conversation.

Kiera sits down in front of me, and I stare a little too closely, trying to tell if something is somehow different about her.

"What are you looking at?" she asks.

"Nothing," I say. "I mean, I was looking at you, and you're not nothing, but . . . sorry." I shake my head. "I spaced out."

I wait for her to say something, but after pausing for a beat, she just nods. "It's cool. I'm feeling kinda spacey too."

"All right, class!" calls Mrs. Young. "We've got a lot of ground to cover this morning. Let's get out those geography books."

A few rows back, Cooper lets out a snort. "Covering ground! Geography. I get it!"

Mrs. Young smirks. "Nice to see someone has a sense of humor bright and early this morning." She claps her hands together. "Let's go, people! You're not in eighth grade yet!"

I reach under my desk for my textbook and try to get Oscar's attention as I do, but I think he's actually doing everything he can not to look in my direction.

As Mrs. Young goes over our chapter review, I tear out a piece of paper from my notebook and jot down a message.

You still mad at me?

I fold the paper up as tiny as I can and write *Oscar* on the outside.

The moment Mrs. Young turns her back to write on the board, I pass the note over to Tyler, who passes it to Greg, who turns to me and smiles before passing it to Oscar. Success!

Oscar holds the note under the palm of his hand before discreetly opening it in his lap. He stares at my message for a minute.

Come on! It's five words! What's there to think about?

He crumples up the paper and coughs into his elbow to cover up the sound.

Oh crud. My stomach sinks.

But then he turns to me and looks me straight in the eyes before shaking his head and mouthing the word *no*.

Relief spreads through my veins.

I give him the thumbs-up.

As we're about to break for lunch, Kiera swivels around to grab a pencil she dropped.

I clear my throat before coughing into my elbow. I've studied her all morning, looking for some kind of difference in her attitude, but the only difference I find is the new lavender beads she added to the ends of her braids. Maybe she hasn't even read the paper yet today.

She reaches into the front zipper of her backpack and hands me a cherry cough drop. "Here," she says.

I take the wax wrapper off. "Thanks." I grin, a little taken aback by her show of goodwill. "Tastes good too."

"Anything to stop you from coughing down my neck and clearing the snot out of your throat. You're not contagious, are you?"

I shrink back a bit. "It's just allergies."

She nods. "I'm sorry," she finally says. "That stinks."

I shove the wrapper in the pocket of my shorts. "Thanks again."

She turns back around without another word and heads off to lunch.

Did . . . Was . . . she . . . I think Kiera Bryant was just nice to me? Maybe a little?

Is this real life?

CHAPTER NINETEEN

Risky Business

After school, I'm not quite ready to go home. It's not that Mom's home or anything like that, but my brain is just buzzing. All I can think about is how my letter—something I wrote all on my own—ran in the *Valentine Gazette*. And when I'm not thinking about that, my brain is in one giant tangle over Kiera.

I take the bus home with Oscar and walk with him to his house.

"You swear you're not mad at me?" I ask again.

He puffs out a sigh. "I'm not mad, but you know if something's going on, you can just tell me."

I hate keeping secrets from Oscar, but for whatever reason, it's impossible for me not to follow Miss Flora Mae's rules. Maybe it's because her advice column is so good, or maybe she really is a vampire and I'm scared of her. But either way, she doesn't want anyone knowing her business. Not even Oscar.

"I know," I say too brightly. "Nothing to report."

With his parents at work, Oscar's house from the hours of three p.m. to five p.m. is a lawless place where anything goes. That probably sounds fun, but when you're the youngest kids in the house, there might as well be a target on your back.

Oscar's middle brother, Jorge, sits on the porch with two of his friends, cracking jokes. "Hey, Sweet Peaches!" he calls.

I roll my eyes. "You know my name," I tell him.

He shrugs. "Whatever." I'd be offended, except that this is almost an inside joke between us at this point, and one time at Green's Grocers last year, Jorge told off an older boy who called me a roly-poly.

"Oscar," he adds. "Coach Herda wants to know if you're coming out for the team."

Oscar scoffs.

"What team?" I whisper.

He shakes his head. "Nothing."

Weird.

We stop in the kitchen so I can call my mom's office

to let her know I'm hanging out here for a little while. I can't wait to start eighth grade and get a cell phone. It's like I'm living in the nineties or something. Aren't parents supposed to want a better life for their kids?

Oscar stands guard, looking over his shoulder every now and then, in the doorway of the kitchen.

"Is everything okay? Where's Luis?" I ask while the line rings.

"I don't know," says Oscar. "And that's the problem. I made the mistake of telling Mom he had a girl in his room with the door closed for a whole hour yesterday after school, and she made us all sit down on the couch last night while she gave us the talk on 'adult choices' she gives the eighth-grade class on their field trip to the clinic, and she grounded Luis too."

"That stinks," I say. I'm grateful for Mrs. Rivera, though. For real. A few months ago, Oscar reached into the front zipper compartment of my backpack looking for a pencil and ended up finding my stash of pads. I was mortified. Oscar might be my BFF, but he's still a boy. Thanks to Mrs. Rivera, who's a nurse at the Valentine Urgent Care, Oscar knew almost more than I did about periods and didn't think it was a big deal.

"I know. And she called the girl's parents, so Luis is definitely out for blood right now."

"I'll be fast," I say just as my mom's office phone goes to voice mail. "Hey, it's me," I say. "I'm hanging out at Oscar's for a little while, and then I'm walking home."

After I dial Dad and leave him the same message, Oscar grabs two watermelon-flavored fizzy waters from the fridge and we run down the hallway to his bedroom.

He swings the door open and there's Luis, stretched across his bed, waiting.

Luis laughs like an old-timey villain. "You didn't think I'd let you sneak in here without going through me, did you?"

Oscar launches his backpack at Luis, but he catches it like he knew all along to expect a flying backpack to the head. If he weren't Oscar's brother, I might even think he was kind of . . . cute? Which is weird . . . because he looks a lot like Oscar.

"It was an accident!" Oscar moans. "Come on. You know it was."

"You got Reyna in serious trouble," Luis says. "And we weren't even doing anything!"

"I didn't say you did."

Luis turns to me, noticing for the first time that I'm here too. "What's up, Sweet Pea?"

I don't really get how to answer that question. Like, do people really want to know what's up? The longer I wait to answer, the warmer my cheeks get. "Nothing," I say. "Just, like, the usual divorced-parents stuff, I guess." *What? Why am I so weird?*

"Cool," he says. "Sorry your parents are still divorced, by the way."

"Oh, it's okay. I think they'll probably stay divorced forever."

"Makes sense." Luis shrugs and then tosses the backpack at Oscar. "Watch your back. The only reason I'm leaving you alone is because Sweet Pea's here."

I bite down on my lips so I don't smile too hard.

Luis walks out and down the hallway to the living room.

Oscar exhales. "You cannot go home before my mom gets here. I forbid it."

I giggle.

"You laugh," he says. "But you've never had two older brothers."

"He's not *really* going to beat you up," I tell him. Oscar's brothers are rough sometimes, but they don't really hurt each other.

His nose wrinkles. "No, but he will fart on my head. Twice. At least. Death by fart attack."

"Don't worry." I pat his arm. "I'm here. You're safe from the fart fumes for now."

We spend the next few hours watching episodes of *America's Most Haunted,* and it's easy to forget I'm hiding anything from my best friend until the next episode starts, and Cliff VanWarren in his spooky yet somehow game-show-announcer voice says, "Secret identities. Not just for comic books, and perhaps more sinister than you may think. You think you know someone only to find they're living a whole other life . . . as a whole other person. The paranormal world—"

I grab the remote and hit the power button. "Sorry," I say. "I gotta go and didn't want it to get any further and spoil the episode."

Oscar throws himself back against the cushions. "Leave me to the fart dungeon, I guess."

"I'm sorry, I'm sorry, I'm sorry, I'm sorry," I sing over and over as I rush out the door.

"Later, Sweet Potatoes!" calls Jorge from where he still sits on the porch with his friends.

"Still Sweet Pea," I shout back. "You'll run out of produce eventually!"

On my way to Dad's, I check on Miss Flora Mae's place. Inside, I plop down on the floor of her plant room and turn on the radio. I sprawl out with the most recent pack of letters from Mr. Joe Salazar and find myself reading through every last one of them.

I've only got a little bit of time before I need to be home, but something about hearing other people's problems makes my own feel farther and farther away. Maybe

that's what Mom likes so much about her job. Some problems make mine feel small and others make them feel
bigger, but for a town so small, there are still an awful lot
of problems.

Arguing siblings, lying significant others, nosy neighbors . . . it goes on and on. Some people just write to ask
Miss Flora Mae about the best way to get rid of a stain in
the couch or what her favorite recipes are. It makes me
wonder how many of these people are just lonely.

I always thought of Miss Flora Mae as this eccentric old
lady who never let anyone in, but maybe that's not true.
Maybe this is her way of letting people in.

There's one letter, though, that I find myself reading
over and over again.

Dear Miss Flora Mae,
My very best friend just moved back home
to Valentine after being gone for over fifteen
years. She left for a new life and never loved
this place the way I have. Some people aren't
meant for small-town life. She promised she'd
call and write, and she did at first, but as her life
changed and mine stayed the same, the phone
stopped ringing and the mailbox sat empty.
Life events have led her back home for a
season, and I want to be there for her. I want

to be the friend she left behind all those years ago, but I can't do the work of being there for her only to experience the pain of being left again. Fool me once. Shame on you. Fool me twice. Shame on me.

Sincerely,
Nobody's Fool

Beside me, the radio crackles as the DJ's voice booms, "And to kick off our commercial-free Thursday night, let's get a little love from Marvin Gaye and Tammi Terrell. 'Ain't No Mountain High Enough.'"

The first few notes play, and a few chimes ring in before a smooth voice croons about mountains and valleys and rivers. A woman's voice scoops in. "If you need me call me, no matter where you are, no matter how far . . ."

I hold the letter close to my chest and sway back and forth to the song while Miss Flora Mae's plants seem to drift along with me, their leaves waving back and forth.

Kiera and I didn't fall apart overnight. Because most things happen a little bit at a time until suddenly you wake up one day and realize things are too different to ignore. My breakup with Kiera started out as tiny cracks until finally it was easier to be rude to each other than it was to pretend to be nice and smooth things over. All the feelings I had about her and her new friends felt too complicated to sift through, and the thought of not knowing where I stood with Kiera was almost worse than her just telling me to get lost. It's like when your cubby at school is such a mess that it's easier to throw everything out than it is to figure out what's worth keeping.

The truth is I never tried to save us. I never stood up for us and the friendship we had.

I stand up with the note still clenched in my fist and take the rest of the letters and the responses I've jotted down so I can type them all. But first I crank up the volume and go sit on Miss Flora Mae's front porch with her cat-eye glasses that you can poke your finger straight through because there are no lenses.

Dear Nobody's Fool,

No one wants to get hurt twice. Sometimes people change, and I guess sometimes they don't, but it sounds like your old friend needs you right now. You might be surprised to find out you need them too.

I wish I could tell you that everything will be fine, but loving people is risky business. Things don't always pan out how we think they should. But I gotta think that when the risk is worth it, it's super worth it.

Sincerely,
Miss Flora Mae

On Friday morning I wake up thinking about the letter I penned last night and how maybe I should follow my own advice. Oscar chatters at me as we walk into school, but my mind is playing the same conversation over and over again in my head.

As we walk into our classroom, we split off in different directions for our desks. "See you at break."

I slide into my chair. Kiera's already sitting there in front of me, concentrating on the daisy she's doodling on her homework folder.

I open my mouth and form the words, but no sound comes out.

I clear my throat and try again.

"Hey, Kiera." My voice sounds so weird, like I've just woken up or something.

I watch over her shoulder as she finishes shading in a leaf. Finally, she turns around.

I expect her to say something like, *Um, yeah?* Or *What do you want?* But she doesn't. She just sits there and waits for me to speak.

She doesn't look like her normal bright self. Her under-eyes are puffy, and her lips are dry and chapped.

"Are you okay?" I ask.

She doesn't look up when she quietly says, "I'd be great if I didn't have to go home and listen to my parents fight all night again."

I don't really know what to say to that. Things haven't been easy with Mom and Dad, but I've never felt like I couldn't bear to go home.

"You can spend the night with me." It's out of my mouth before I even have a second to realize what a huge mistake I've made. Kiera. Spending the night. At my house. What was I thinking?

She studies me for a minute and I kind of wonder if she's trying to give me a chance to take it back. "At your house?"

"Well, one of them. I'm at my dad's house tonight." Oh crud. And tonight's my dad's night. What if her dad has to drop her off or, even worse, what if he says she can't spend the night?

This was a terrible idea. Asking someone to spend the night is like the highest level of friendship. You have to totally trust them. Because what if they hear you fart in your sleep? Or find out you have to cover your body in zit cream before bed every night? Or what if your parents let embarrassing stories slip? Basically, anything and everything could go wrong.

She pauses, and her eyes dart from side to side, like she's about to cross the street. "I guess it's better than being at home right now."

I'm not really sure what to say to that. "Oscar will probably be there too."

"Okay," she says.

"So that's a yes?" I ask, practically holding my breath.

"Sure."

Yup. I'm dead. Totally for sure dead.

CHAPTER TWENTY

No Right Choice

After school, Dad is sitting at the kitchen table in his dirty old painting overalls, which would drive Mom nuts. It's kind of funny to see all the things Dad does differently when Mom's not around to have things her way. Like the silverware. He keeps it all the way on the other side of the kitchen. And he doesn't organize his cups. Just puts them in any which way.

"Hey, Sweet Pea," he says as I walk in. "I just got a, uh, interesting phone call from Mrs. Bryant."

I hate the idea of Kiera not being allowed to come over just because of her dad, but I've also kind of had my fingers crossed all day that something would happen and she wouldn't be able to come over. I sit down across from him with my backpack still on. "Uh. Okay."

"Well, she says Kiera's spending the night here tonight."

"Um, yeah. About that . . . I totally forgot to check with you first. I'm so sorry. It was kind of an in-the-moment thing when I invited her."

He nods. "It's okay. I let Mrs. Bryant think I knew." I want to ask about Kiera's dad and what he had to say about Kiera spending the night here. But I don't know how to bring it up without making things awkward. I wasn't supposed to know about the big fight Dad and Mr. Bryant got into. But I heard him and Mom talking about it at the kitchen table after Dad had moved out. He came over late one night and I think I even heard him cry. Just the *thought* of Dad crying made me cry too.

"I played it totally cool," he continues. "But she did say that Kiera wouldn't be allowed to sleep over if there was a boy here."

"What?" I ask. "It's Oscar. Why do people have to make such a big deal about boy-and-girl stuff? He's my friend. If we wanted to do . . . ya know, stuff, I'm pretty sure it wouldn't take a sleepover for that to happen."

Dad shrugs and shakes his head, like he's trying to rid himself of the thought of me + a boy + doing stuff. "I hear you loud and clear, Sweet Pea. I'm not saying you're wrong. And I'm happy to have the two of them over, but if you want to play by Mrs. Bryant's rules, you gotta choose one or the other." He stands up and knocks the top of the table with his fist. "I'm gonna hop in the shower. Kiera's number is on the fridge. You let me know what you decide."

I shake my head. "Yeah. Okay."

I plop my elbows down on the table and cradle my face in my hands. This just stinks.

At first, I think the clear choice is Oscar. But the more I think about it, the more I realize there's no good answer.

I feel just sick with guilt every time I think about how down Kiera was today. Maybe she's just using me to get away from her parents, but what if we could go back to the way things were? And Oscar . . . well, he's my best friend until the end of forever. No way could I ditch him like this. But then again, Oscar comes over every Friday, so maybe it's okay for us to take a weekend off. And maybe it is kind of weird to have a boy spend the night at my house every Friday. I don't know.

Either way, I'm running out of time to make a choice. I reach for the phone on the counter and punch a number into the keypad.

A voice answers on the third ring. "Sweet Pea!"

"Mrs. Rivera?"

She laughs. "I certainly hope so! When are we going to see you over here again?"

"Oh, trust me," I say. "I've got a whole bunch of nothing planned this summer, so you won't be able to get rid of me."

She tsks into the phone. "You're not signed up for any extracurricular activities yet? Lots of those run through the summer. I've got Oscar signing up for all kinds of clubs and even wrestling, I think."

"What? Oscar signed up for wrestling?" Oscar avoids sweating as much as I do, and he hates when his brothers horse around. Why would he sign up for wrestling?

"I could've sworn he gave me the schedule." I can hear her shuffling through papers. "You'll have to ask him yourself, hon. I've got paper coming out of my ears over here."

"Speaking of, could I talk to Oscar?"

"Just a moment!" She muffles the receiver, but the speaker still crackles when she shouts, "Mijo!"

A few seconds later, Oscar sighs into the phone. "I've got it, Mom!"

"Hey, it's me," I say. "Your mom said something about you signing up for clubs? And a sport even?"

I can hear him chewing on his lip—his nervous tic. "Yeah, we can talk about it tonight. My mom's getting my brother to give me a ride later. What time should I come over?"

"Well, I sort of have some bad news. . . ." And then I lay

it all out for him, and to my surprise, Mrs. Bryant's dumb rule is the least of his concerns.

"You invited *Kiera* to our sleepover without even asking me first?"

I groan. "I don't know. I mean, yes. But you dragged me to her birthday party. How was I supposed to know you'd even care?"

"I didn't make you go to her party. You wanted to check out Trampoline Zone as much as I did."

"I just . . . we used to be such good friends. And she's going through a lot right now."

"What is she going through?" he asks.

"It's really not for me to say."

"Whatever, Sweet Pea. So I guess Little Miss I-Get-Everything-I-Want Kiera is going through   something. And so all of a sudden after she just mysteriously ditched you for years, you've invited her to our sleepover and in doing so have uninvited me?"

"Well, when you put it like that . . ." I sigh into the receiver. "Oscar, just trust me on this, please? I'm so, so sorry. And I owe you so big-time. I promise to make it up to you."

"Yeah, you've been promising lots of things lately."

"I really will make it up to you."

"Whatever," he says.

165

"So we're cool?"

"I don't know, Sweet Pea. Sure. I guess so."

I squeal into the phone. "You're the best, you're the best, you're the best. I promise I really will make it up to you. Me. You. Trampoline Zone. Zero puke. I'll even use my allowance to pay for us both. And—and I'll buy you the fancy socks they sell."

"Whatever you say," he says flatly. "Have fun at your slumber party."

I'm feeling guilty and annoyed all at once. Guilty that I had to choose Kiera over Oscar and annoyed that I can't make Oscar understand why.

After we hang up, the light on the phone is blinking red. I hit the voice-mail number next to the light. We never really get voice messages since anything important goes to Mom's or Dad's phones. I'm sure this message is just some fake spam message saying we won a cruise to Alaska or something.

"Andre? Andre DiMarco? This is Saul Benson from Liberty Finance up in Bridgeport, Connecticut. I was calling about that small-business loan we discussed. We got you approved. Sent out a letter in the mail. I tried to connect via email, but looks like I got your address wrong and the email bounced back. Give me a call when you can. We gotta tie up some loose ends and get you up here to get some things in order. Anyway, listen, give me a call back.

And congrats! Can't wait to get you on your feet with the shop."

A new shop? And it's in Connecticut? I don't get it. Would Dad really move halfway across the country without talking to me first? My stomach plummets.

"To save this message, press nine. To delete this message, press zero."

I pull the phone away from my ear. My fingers hover for a minute over the keypad.

Zero. Zero, zero, zero, zero. I can't press it enough times.

CHAPTER TWENTY-ONE

The Kind of Promise You Can Keep

That night, Kiera's mom walks her to the door and spends about a good thirty seconds apologizing to Dad about the whole Oscar "fiasco" and another ten minutes explaining to Dad about why this age is so "delicate" and how our bodies are changing.

The whole thing is about as entertaining as watching ice melt, so Kiera and I head to my room and let Dad take one for the team. As we're walking down the hall, I hear Mrs. Bryant pause and say, "And Andre, I also wanted to say that I'm sorry about Nate and uh . . . the whole—"

Dad interrupts her. "Thanks, Shawna."

Kiera and I look at each other for a moment and then

look away. I don't really know how to talk about her dad, and I don't think she does either.

I open my door, and Kiera follows me inside.

"Whoa," says Kiera as she drops her backpack on my bed. "This is, like, basically what I remember your room looking like when y'all all lived together." She turns to me. "Is this the same wallpaper?"

"Look closer," I tell her.

She runs her fingers over the peach-colored walls and sees that the little pattern is completely painted by hand.

"This is painted?" she asks.

I nod. "Dad couldn't find the matching paper, so he just painted it himself."

She shakes her head in disbelief. "That's kind of weird, but it's really sweet too."

I plop down in my desk chair. "It is, isn't it?"

"I can't believe how much this place looks like your other room. It's like a museum, kind of. It's like they never even got a divorce."

"That's sort of the point, I think."

"What do you mean?"

"My mom calls it mirror houses. She didn't want things to change for me too much, so she got my dad to rent this place and make it up to look almost like the old house. But there are still some differences if you look closely. A lot, actually."

She turns around, looking at every detail. "Weird."

"You're not kidding."

"But, like, is this house the exact same with all the same rooms and everything?"

I shake my head. "Not quite. Mom's house has two bedrooms and this one has a third."

"What does your dad keep in it?"

"Huh." I think for a moment. "I've never actually been in there."

"Can we go in there now?"

"Um, I don't know." I've convinced myself that whatever is behind that door is no big deal, but the way Kiera is pushing the issue makes me uneasy.

"It's your house, isn't it?"

I can't help but feel a little defensive. Of course it's my house. "I think it's just his old stuff. Maybe later." I clear my throat. "Um, so you know what your mom was talking about out there, right?"

"About my dad and your dad?"

"And how my dad is gay now." I force my shoulders straight as I say it, just in case Kiera agrees more with her dad than her mom.

"What do you mean *now*? Isn't that the kind of thing where you're that way the whole time?"

I hold my hands up and shrug, a little relieved by her reaction. "I'm not really sure how all this works."

She doesn't really have much to say to that, so she loops her fingers through the carpet and says, "I heard my parents arguing about it. Your dad," she clarifies. "As if they didn't already have enough to argue about."

I prickle at that. It's not my dad's fault that her parents are fighting. "I'm sorry, I guess? Maybe if your dad wasn't . . . Never mind."

"Wasn't what?" she asks, daring me to finish my sentence.

My throat dries up and sweat gathers between my fingers. This is definitely going as bad as I expected. "Wasn't such a jerk," I finish in a low voice.

Her gaze narrows in on me. Then she brushes me off with a wave of her hand. "Mom says it's none of our business and that it shouldn't change anything. Especially if your mom is so okay with it."

"I wouldn't say she's okay with it, but she's not mad at him." I pull my knees up to my chest and hold them there while I think of the right way to explain. "She knows he doesn't mean to hurt us, but it's kind of hard, because I think it might be easier if they didn't like each other so much and just got divorced for the usual reasons."

"You wanna borrow my parents?" she asks. "They've got no problem blaming each other."

I laugh. It's the kind of thing that only kids with messed-up parents can laugh at, like some awful inside joke, but at least it's a reminder that you're not alone.

And then Kiera starts to laugh too.

I stand up, feeling suddenly better about the whole night. "You wanna watch some TV? My dad said we can order pizza."

"Are you going to puke it all over the place?" she teases.

I roll my eyes. "Come on," I say. "Can you not with the puke jokes?"

She cracks a smile. "That was my last one, I swear."

We settle into the couch to watch an episode of *Girl Meets World*, and it's no *America's Most Haunted*, but it'll do.

After the pizza comes, Dad joins us, and we all eat around the coffee table. Dad and I watch in confusion as Kiera pats down her slice with a napkin.

"What?" she asks when she catches us staring. "Grease makes you fat."

I put my pizza back down on my plate. I hate when people say stuff like that. It makes me queasy and angry at the same time. It's like she's not even thinking before she talks. Or like she doesn't even *see* me.

I'd be lying if I said this wasn't the first time I wondered if part of the reason Kiera ditched me was because she was tired of being friends with the fat girl. I saw in one of Mom's magazines once a diagram of all the different shapes women are supposed to be, and they didn't really have anything that looked like my body, because no one in magazines writes about girls who are shaped like oranges with Popsicle sticks for legs. I'm okay with who I am and what I look like, or at least I try to be. I just wish people, Kiera included, would feel the same way.

Dad takes a huge bite of pizza. "Around here neither of those words—grease or fat—are a bad thing."

A warm glow radiates in my chest, and I feel immediately guilty for erasing Dad's voice mail. It's like there's a bright neon sign above my head with an arrow pointing right on me. *Worst Daughter of the Year.*

Sometimes Dad just knows how to tell someone they're wrong without making anyone feel weird. Like when the furniture delivery guys were bringing his coffee table in, and one of them made a pretty cheesy joke. The other guy said, "That's so gay, man."

Dad didn't skip a beat when he said, "That joke was bad. Not gay."

The guys were quiet at first, but just laughed it off. When I asked him what he meant by that, he just said, "Sometimes people use the word *gay* to mean a negative thing, but there's nothing wrong with the word *gay* or the people who use it to identify themselves. Trust me. I've got plenty of issues—your mom would agree—but being gay isn't one of them."

It was as simple as that. Sometimes I think that about the word *fat*. Maybe it doesn't have to be a bad thing.

"Sorry," Kiera says to Dad. She looks to me. "I didn't mean anything by it."

"Words mean things," I say, and take a bite out of my slice. "It's okay, though. Thanks."

She nods and quietly eats the rest of her pizza, still patting away the grease every once in a while, but not making a big deal of it.

I wonder what Oscar is doing right now and if his night is half as awkward as mine or if Luis is farting on his head at this very moment.

After we watch a few episodes of *Stranger Things*, the only show me, Kiera, and Dad can all agree on, Dad heads to bed and leaves me and Kiera on our own. We change into our pajamas and Kiera wraps her braids into a silk polka-dot scarf; the two of us sprawl out in the living room—me on the big couch and her on the love seat—and flip through channels before landing on a mesmerizing infomercial about a portable snow-cone machine.

"When did you know your parents were gonna get divorced?" Kiera asks.

I roll over onto my stomach, so I can face her. "When they told me."

"You mean you didn't know? You didn't see it coming?"

I shake my head. "Not even a little bit." I can't disguise how glum it makes me feel. I want Mom and Dad to be happy. I just wish it involved them being together. "My mom's a therapist, and *she* didn't even see it coming."

"My mom always talks about how smart your mom is."

I can't stop myself from smiling. Sometimes I get so used to Mom just being Mom that I forget how smart and good at her job she really is. Even if I don't love this idea of identical houses, she helps lots of people in Valentine.

"Afterward, though," I continue, "when she thought about it, she could see that something was missing for Dad. Sometimes I think Dad would have just kept things the way they were and that he'd be happy to live with us if him and Mom could just be, like, roommates."

"If I were your mom, I'd think that'd be even worse."

I nod along, even though I can't help but secretly wish that things had played out that way. Because I'm selfish and I don't care if they're in love. I only cared that they were together. For me.

"Wow," says Kiera, her voice breathy. "I almost think that might be worse than all the fighting my parents are doing. I don't know what's gonna happen with them, but if they do split, maybe I'll at least be relieved that they won't be having nonstop screaming matches across the house."

"My turn to ask a question," I say.

She shrugs. "Okay."

I swallow back my fears. Part of me doesn't want to hear

this answer, and the other part is too chicken to ask. "Me and you. What happened?" I shake my head. "It was like one day you woke up and decided I wasn't friend material anymore."

Kiera groans so low that it almost sounds like a growl. She sits up. "I'm trying to think of a way to say this without sounding like a jerk."

"Well, that's not great." Regret and nerves take hold of me. This whole night is about to turn sour really quick.

She looks to me with something that feels like pity, but it's not mean-spirited or gloating. Just like she plain old feels bad. "You were my best friend, okay? But things started to change. Not things! We! Us! We started to change. I wanted to make more friends, and it's like all you cared about was little-kid stuff. How was I supposed to stay friends with you when all you cared about was little-kid stuff?"

"You liked plenty of little-kid things too. And why is that even a bad thing, anyway?"

"I don't know, Sweet Pea. I wanted more friends. You never really liked letting people into our circle."

"If by 'more friends,' you mean prettier friends. Skinnier friends." Something about saying it out loud stings more than I expected.

She rolls her eyes. "You're pretty, Sweet Pea."

"That's not the point! It shouldn't matter if I am or not.

For the record, I don't think I'm ugly, but it was like you started caring about lip gloss and boys and popularity, and maybe I wanted to care about those things too. Or maybe I didn't. I don't know."

"I'm not saying it was the right thing to do or trying to make any excuses, okay? Really, I'm not. But, like, Sarah Beth, Claire, and Kassidy didn't really click with you, okay?"

I cringe at their names. Sarah Beth, Claire, and Kassidy, her older friends, who are in secondary school now. All three of them went out of their way to let me know how unwelcome I was. Playing pranks on me in the middle of the night at sleepovers and having private conversations in Kiera's closet after everyone had pretended to go to sleep, leaving only me on the floor of Kiera's room in my sleeping bag. "Well, where are Sarah Beth, Claire, and Kassidy now? Huh?"

She winces. "We're still friends."

"They weren't at your birthday party."

"They've been busy with eighth-grade stuff," she mutters. "It's different there. Anyway, you were so busy with Oscar!"

"Who you wouldn't even try being friends with," I remind her.

"It felt like he was always trying to compete for your attention," she says.

"Are Sarah Beth, Claire, and Kassidy really that busy that they can't even make time for your birthday party?" I ask.

She throws herself back against the love seat and groans. "They said it was a little-kid party. I never see them anyway since they started eighth grade, and they're busy all the time with, like, clubs, and I think Sarah Beth has a new boyfriend. I don't know."

"A *second* boyfriend? That's probably more than I'll have in my whole lifetime."

Kiera snorts. "Me and you both."

We both laugh, our shoulders bumping together until we've quieted down and are watching the ceiling fan spin above us. I have one more question. "So now that your cool older friends are too busy for you, you're ready to be friends again?"

"I'm not perfect, okay? I've wanted to talk to you for basically the whole year. But I didn't know how to make things go back to the way they were. It's not like you were trying to be my friend either."

"What about eighth grade?" I ask, remembering the letter I responded to last night. "What if we just change too much again?"

Kiera looks at me, like every bone in her body is as serious as can be, and I think this is what I like most about her. "A lot of things have happened that I never thought would happen. Your parents got a divorce. Mine are on the verge of strangling each other, and Cooper won the class spelling bee even though he misspelled his own name on his cubby. So I bet we'll change a lot in the next few years and even more before we graduate twelfth grade, but we can try to do it together. If you want?"

Most people would probably turn to me and promise me that things would never change. But Kiera never makes promises she can't keep. And who knows what will happen, anyway? What Kiera's offering, though, feels like the kind of promise we could keep. "Yeah." I nod. "I'd like that."

"Enough with all this serious talk," she says. "Can we finally check out your dad's spare bedroom? I want to know what he's hiding."

I suck in a deep breath. I don't feel so good about this. "Sure," I finally say. "But it's probably nothing." At least I hope so.

CHAPTER TWENTY-TWO

Behind Door Number Three

I'm just as curious as Kiera—if not more curious—but some weird part of me would rather not know what's behind the door of Dad's mystery room. It's like the same way my nerves are on the fritz every time I go to the doctor, because I'm scared they're going to tell me I've got some incurable rare disease. And if I do . . . honestly? I'd just rather not know.

But curiosity and peer pressure win out, so after pressing my ear to my dad's door to make sure he's asleep, I wave Kiera down the hall.

When I make no move to open the door, Kiera reaches out and turns the doorknob. We're greeted by a pitch-black room, so she takes the lead and feels her way along the wall until she finds a light switch.

Whoa.

I don't know what I expected, but this is not it.

It's like an art studio. Full of easels and paint with canvases propped up against the wall and the drop cloth Dad uses at his job during the day to protect the floors.

Kiera steps ahead of me to take a look around. "I knew your dad was a painter, Sweet Pea, but I didn't know he was a *painter.*"

And he is. He really is. I wondered what Dad might be doing over here in all the hours he'd always filled with me and Mom. Now I see. Paintings of me. Me with Cheese. Grandma. Even a woman who looks like Miss Flora Mae. All of them with bright, popping backgrounds. Lime green. Fluorescent purple. Blinding yellow.

They're not art-museum good (actually, I've never been to a real art museum, so what do I know?), but they're good in a different kind of way. One canvas leaning against the wall is the only one not of a person or Cheese. This one is two identical houses side by side. No house in between. It's the perfect-world version of my mom's mirror-house plan.

"Hey!" says Kiera. "I love this one of you and Cheese!"

She holds up a canvas, and sure enough it's me. Waves tamed into curls, black-and-white-striped turtleneck, my favorite black corduroy skirt, and a double chin. I'm sitting on a wooden chair, and Cheese sits curled in my lap. The background is a bright mustard yellow that fades at the edges into the white of the canvas.

My cheeks blush at the sight of myself. I see all the details that stand out to Dad when he looks at me—my hair, my smile, my eyes. It's like I'm seeing myself through someone else's eyes. The most artistic things I'd ever seen Dad do were his seasonal window paintings, and those were mostly turkeys or peppermint wheels, but this is real, actual art. "Wow. This is . . ."

"Beautiful," Kiera finishes.

I nod. "It is."

After we do a little more snooping around, we're sure to leave everything just as we found it. We head back to my room, and Kiera and I decide to share my bed. One difference between Mom's and Dad's houses is that at Dad's I have a bigger bed with plenty of room to share.

As we lie there, waiting to fall asleep, I think about telling Kiera about Miss Flora Mae and maybe even fessing up about the letter to her that I responded to.

But just as I open my mouth, Kiera says, "I can't believe your dad has kept that room all shut off and hasn't told you about it."

For a moment, I feel bad, like he doesn't trust me enough or that I won't understand, but then I think about how I feel when I have to do any kind of artwork at school. "Maybe he's embarrassed."

She nods vigorously, casting a shadow on the wall. "Artsy people can be funny about that stuff. My aunt Simone makes pottery, and she gets real touchy about people going into her studio or seeing any of her work before it's done."

"That makes sense." And then after a moment, I say what I'm scared to even think. "But what if he felt like he couldn't paint when we all lived together? Like, what if he's just now painting because it's like he's free of me and Mom? He can finally be the person he's always wanted to be."

Kiera rolls over to face me. "I don't know, Sweet Pea, but if that's true, I think that's his problem and not yours."

I want to believe her and for that to be true, but I can't help but think of the voice mail I deleted today and all the big plans it sounds like Dad has. Maybe that's all he needed. Space from Mom. From us. And now he can do and be all the things he always dreamed of. Without us. Without me.

CHAPTER TWENTY-THREE

Common Ground

The next morning is wet and gray, and Mr. Bryant picks up Kiera after his bowling league. When Dad spots his truck from the kitchen, he turns to me and says, "Sweet Pea, why don't you take the umbrella and walk Kiera out to her dad's truck so he doesn't have to get out in this weather?"

"Sure thing, Dad." I slip on my sneakers and am careful not to open the umbrella inside (bad luck and all that). Kiera and I don't have to say it out loud to know that Dad sending us out here by ourselves has nothing to do with not making Mr. Bryant trudge up the walkway in the rain.

"I had a good time," Kiera tells me.

Her dad reaches across the truck to open her door. The rain is coming sideways now. Part of me wants to double-check that she really did have fun and that she's sure she wants to be friends again. But my butt is already soaked from the rain, so I just say, "Me too."

Mr. Bryant gives me a short wave and a nod, and in a gravelly voice says, "Nice to see you, Sweet Pea."

I run back inside and splash through the big puddle before the front door, because even if Mr. Bryant is a royal jerk, I'm still in a great mood.

On Sunday night, after I finish up my homework, I sneak out while Dad is cooking dinner to package up Miss Flora Mae's new letters.

As I skip through the living room around to the back to water the plants, I wave in the general direction of the mantel. "Hey there, Bette Davis!"

While I put together the envelope for Miss Flora Mae, I play some music for the plants and find myself swaying along to a man named Otis Redding singing about sitting on a dock. I slide each letter into the large manila envelope and I hold the last one there in my hand for a moment. There's some kind of rush I can't quite explain that I got from responding to Kiera. And it wasn't just because I knew her situation so well. I liked the idea of helping someone, and to be honest, it kind of made me understand why my mom takes her job so gosh darn seriously.

On Monday morning, I settle into my desk. I try waving at Oscar, but I think he's doing everything in his power not to look in my direction. I tried calling him over the weekend, but every time either Luis or Jorge picked up the phone and said Oscar was busy. Busy with what? His new career on the wrestling team that he has yet to tell me about?

"All right, class!" Mrs. Young claps her hands to get our attention. "Before we get going for the day, I want to remind you all of your last assignment before finals."

The class simultaneously groans. Our dreaded research presentation. Even though Mrs. Young assigned it back in April, I've been putting it off this whole time, and from the looks of it, I'm not the only one.

She's unfazed. "Before I can let you move on to your new life as eighth graders, you've got one last hurdle to jump."

Someone at the back of the class mumbles, "I don't jump hurdles. I've got a doctor's note."

"The seventh-grade research project!" Mrs. Young says, as if any of us could forget. "On any prominent figure you like. Living or dead. Now, remember, they can be YouTube stars or singers or artists or engineers or web designers. As long as you can find actual bona fide research on them using the tools we learned about during our weekly trips to the school library."

The class begins to buzz with possibilities. No one likes doing a project, but the thought of getting to choose anyone and not just another dusty old white guy? That's pretty cool.

"Presentations will be given verbally next week just before our social studies final. You have until next Monday to let me know whom you'll be presenting on," she finishes.

Kiera swivels around. "Dibs on Jungkook."

"On who?" I ask.

She gives me a swoony sigh. "Only the dreamiest member of BTS. Honestly, it's too late for you to even call dibs, because I've been working on this project for weeks."

"BTS?" She is literally speaking another language right now.

"BTS," she says. "The K-pop band? Ya know, Korean pop music?"

"No comprende," I tell her. From the corner of my eye, I see Oscar watching us from across the room. We've been talking, but things just feel weird, and I'm sure him seeing me and Kiera all buddy-buddy isn't helping.

She giggles before turning back around. "I have so much to teach you."

She's right. There's so much I don't know. But right now what I really don't know is who the heck I'm going to pick for my project.

I end up spending time at Miss Flora Mae's house on Monday and then again on Tuesday. I snuck another response from me into this week's package for Mr. Joe Salazar. So if I'm doing my math right, my next published letter should be in this Thursday's paper.

On Wednesday, there's another fresh batch of letters waiting for me in the mailbox, and I run inside, water the plants, turn on the radio, wave to Bette Davis the cat, and tear into the latest letters.

With a fizzing glass of ginger ale in hand, I find that the letters have a way of blending together. It's not that they're boring, but it's just a surprise to see how much everyone has in common and how alike all our problems really are.

Some of the letters are pretty funny. One guy is about to move in with his girlfriend and is scared of farting in his sleep. I decide to write him back, taking a page out of Mom's book when I remind him that sometimes bodies are just bodies. I assure him that farting is totally normal.

Another woman writes in asking for tips on how to get her cat to learn how to use and flush the toilet. One lady wants to know if it's polite to try to bargain with the guy behind the deli counter, and one guy even sent in a picture of a mole shaped like Mickey Mouse, wondering if it was too cool to get rid of or if he should let his dermatologist remove it. I leave all of those for Miss Flora Mae.

My favorite, though, is one I can't resist answering.

Dear Miss Flora Mae,

I start kindergarten next year, and I'm so nervous that I haven't been able to sleep. My mom said maybe you would have advice. In fact, she's the one writing you for me. I hope that's okay.

Sincerely,

Little Miss Nervous

P.S. Hi, Miss Flora Mae!—Little Miss Nervous's Equally Nervous Mom

This is the first letter that I've read that I not only relate to, but I've been there. Maybe I've found my calling in giving advice. Mom always said I had a bossy streak.

Dear Little Miss Nervous,

I've been there. We all have. Starting a new thing is always scary. No more naps and snacks whenever you feel like it and no parents there to make you feel safe. The first thing you should know is that everyone else is just as nervous as you are. The second thing you should know is that you have way more reason to be excited than nervous. There's no guarantee that every day of the school year will be awesome, but most things aren't all good or all bad. Enjoy the good days and learn from the tough ones. But most importantly of all: don't trade lunch with anyone who eats peanut butter on their ham sandwich. I made that mistake once, and it only took one time to learn my lesson.

Sincerely,

Miss Flora Mae

And for the first time, it really hurts me to type her name and not my own, because this is one I want to take credit for.

When I get home to Mom's, she and Dad are sitting on the couch, laughing at some awful pun the weatherman just made about our chances of rain this week.

"What are y'all doing?" I ask. It takes a whole lot of self-control to not remind them that they're divorced.

They both turn around and Mom says, "We thought we could use a family night out."

"Huh?" I drop my backpack on the kitchen table. "Like, all three of us? On a school night?"

Dad half smiles. "We're still a family, Sweet Pea. We just are—"

"We've taken a new shape," finishes Mom.

Dad nods. "Exactly. And tonight we thought we'd take the shape of a bowling league. What do you say?"

Dad's always been the bowler in the family, and I'm no good without bumpers. The last time they made a big effort for all three of us to be together, they told me they were getting a divorce, so it's hard not to wonder what bad news awaits me. That's not enough to stop me from saying, "Winner buys me a few rounds on the crane machines!"

That night, Dad goes easy on us, but he can't stop himself from scoring a few strikes. We order nachos and burgers and share a slushy that's bigger than my head.

After a few failed attempts at the crane machines, the three of us file out to Dad's truck. We all slide in with me in the middle, and I'm so wiped I can barely keep my head up. I slouch against Mom's shoulder and declare, "I must be French, because I'm fried!"

On the way home, I fall in and out of sleep and both Mom and Dad help me into bed and tuck me in. I wait and wait for the bad news to come, but it never does.

CHAPTER TWENTY-FOUR

Back on the Market

When the paper comes again on Thursday, I play it cool. But I am totally dying to see my second response published.

After I get dressed for school, I check the front porch for the paper.

"Looking for this?" asks Mom, grinning as she waves the paper around like she's trying to tempt me.

"Come on," she says. "Let's read this thing over breakfast. But first I need to talk to you."

"Okay." I'm automatically suspicious.

I sit down to scrambled eggs and s'mores Pop-Tarts. Dad was definitely the breakfast chef.

She waits for me to dig in. Probably so that my mouth

is too full to fight back when she drops whatever news she's sitting on.

"Do you remember a few weeks ago when I met up with someone for drinks after book club?" She speaks slowly, like she's nervous.

"Uh-huh."

"Well, I've been talking to that person a lot recently."

So that explains all the giggling into her phone lately.

"You mean like a friend?"

She blushes. "No, baby. I've started dating someone."

"Like, you have a boyfriend?" My voice goes high. And I think I could puke. It didn't even take pizza, cake, and a whole gymnasium full of trampolines.

A slow blush gathers on her cheeks. "Well, I wouldn't say he's my boyfriend, but I do like him very much."

This is too weird. And wrong in so many ways! How could she just be over Dad so quickly? Didn't their marriage mean anything to her? Anger begins to build up inside of me. She's probably ready to start from scratch with a whole new family.

"Things are just casual right now, but I just wanted you to know."

"Casual? What does that even mean?"

She gives me a patient smile. "It just means that we're not making a big deal of anything. Nothing's official or too serious. And you and I can talk about it as much or as little as you want. I understand if you're not ready, and I wouldn't blame you," she says in full therapist voice. "But you can ask questions whenever you want."

"Does he have a name?" I ask bitterly.

"His name is Sam. Sam Reyes. He has a really lovely daughter who's about to be a senior over at Clover City High. Her name is Callie."

"How did you meet?"

"We have a few mutual friends. I actually know his mom from when I'd go for trainings at the University of Texas in El Paso, and she introduced us."

I want nothing more than to talk to Oscar about all of this ASAP, but I'm not exactly on his good side right now. He's been talking to me, but only using a few sarcastic words at a time. "Do I have to meet him?" I ask Mom, returning my attention to her dating life. Ugh.

She laughs, and I think part of it is all the nerves that must have been raveled up inside her. "Only when you're ready."

I don't know why, but I somehow felt Dad would find someone first and I definitely didn't think it would be . . . "So soon," I find myself saying.

Mom's expression turns serious. "It's early," she says. "I know. But I think if this divorce has taught me anything, it's that none of us should waste any time waiting for happiness. Not if we can go out there and take it for ourselves."

I sit there in disbelief. I don't even know what to say. And I especially don't know what she expects me to say.

"I wasn't looking for anyone, Sweet Pea. It just sort of happened."

I take a sip of my orange juice and then a bite of eggs. I'll stuff my face with anything if it will just end this conversation as quick as possible. I think about Dad and his big plans and his secret painting room and how happy he seems to be. What about Mom? When does she get to be happy? And at least she's including me. That's more than I can say for Dad.

Mom cracks open the paper and shakes it out, opening right up to *Miss Flora Mae I?* She lets out a delighted chuckle. "Oh, how sweet is this! A letter from a little one nervous about going to kindergarten. Would you like to read it, or shall I?"

I almost can't remember what it felt like to be excited about reading my latest published letter today. "You can," I tell her. "I like it when you read to me."

CHAPTER TWENTY-FIVE

Let It All Out

Let's recap. My parents are divorced. My dad is gay, and my mom has a new boyfriend. She's not calling him her boyfriend yet, but he's totally her boyfriend. I'm pretending to be the town advice columnist while the regular advice lady is MIA. My best friend is ticked off at me, and I've somehow managed to become friends again with my once-sworn enemy.

I need a vacation.

"Are you sure you can't take me with you?" I ask Kiera, only half joking.

"Trust me," she says over the constant buzz of conversation in the lunch room. "You want nothing to do with my family gatherings right now."

"How old is your great-grandma?"

"She's going to be a hundred and four," she says.

Oscar sits across from us, hunched over his turkey sandwich. Yesterday he actually chose to sit with us, so maybe he's making baby steps.

"And you have to go all the way to San Antonio this weekend?"

"I guess you only turn a hundred and four once," says Kiera.

"When exactly do you leave again?" asks Oscar. "Any minute now, right?"

I shoot him a look.

"What?" he asks. "It's a long drive."

Kiera tosses her braids back. "My parents are picking me up after lunch."

What do you do when your friends refuse to be friends with each other? I can't blame Oscar. We spent a lot of time together talking about all the reasons Kiera was awful. And Kiera's not exactly making it easier either.

The awkward silence radiating from the two of them hangs over my head like a fog. I search for something— anything!—to make it stop. On the other side of Kiera, Cooper and Greg sit hovered over Cooper's new phone.

"Hey, Greg," I say, interrupting them.

He turns to me with a look of confusion. "Uh, yeah?"

"So are you going to be around this summer?"

He perks up. "I might be spending some time with my aunt."

"Oh yeah. I remember you talking about her in class. Isn't she a park ranger or something?"

He nods. "Yeah, out in Big Bend. She runs an astronomy camp out there, which would be cool, but I don't really know if I'm going yet. I kind of wouldn't mind hanging out around here this summer, too, ya know? Maybe take some lifeguard classes so I can work at the pool."

"You can't be a real lifeguard until you're sixteen," Oscar points out unhelpfully.

I nudge Oscar in the ribs. "I mean, both of those plans sound really cool."

Next to Greg, Cooper rolls his eyes. "Did you need something? We were in the middle of a conversation."

"Whoa," says Kiera. "Attitude much, Coop? The most interesting thing you've ever been in the middle of is all the cow poop on your parents' farm."

"Hey," says Cooper. "Everybody poops."

"Nice one," says Oscar to Kiera, surprising even himself.

Kiera looks past me at Oscar skeptically, but then realizes he was being serious. "Thanks."

I shake my head. Common enemies, according to Cliff VanWarren, are the great unifier.

Greg gives me a *rescue me* smile and shrugs before turning back to Cooper.

Without much else to say, I turn to Oscar. "So, Oscar, are we on for tonight?"

He makes a low hissing noise as he sucks in through his teeth. "Yeah. Tonight doesn't really *work* for me." He says it like I'm asking him if he likes stripes or plaid. *Patterns don't really work for me.*

The lunch bell rings, and everyone begins to stand and gather up their trash. "What? How come?"

An office aide scoops up Kiera because her parents are here. "See you on Monday!" I call to her as I follow Oscar to the trash cans.

"You come over every Friday night," I remind him.

He dumps his leftovers in the trash and turns around. "Not every Friday night," he says.

"Are you still mad about the Kiera thing?" I ask, my hands on my hips. "I think y'all would actually get along if you just tried."

He ignores my question. "I just can't tonight."

"Well, why not?"

"Because, Sweet Pea. I don't know. Maybe I have other plans, okay? We don't have to spend every Friday night together. Besides, my brothers say it's weird how much we hang out, and maybe they're right."

"I wouldn't exactly trust your brothers to be experts on girls and guys being best friends."

Oscar stops in his tracks. "I just can't this weekend. You're making this into a bigger deal than it is."

My chest tightens, and I can feel tears welling up, but I refuse to let him see me cry right now. For the first time I can remember, I feel silly for caring so much about this. He clearly doesn't. It's like when everyone is in on a joke and you're the last person to realize everyone else has stopped playing along. "Okay, fine," I tell him. "Totally cool. We'll hang out next week. Maybe after school one day."

Oscar nods. "Cool."

Later that day, after I get off the bus, I stop at Mom's house to see Cheese even though it's Dad's night. I lie next to him on the kitchen floor, dangling a string in front of his nose as he bats it back and forth.

I barely notice as it gets darker, the sun sinking lower into the sky outside.

The front door creaks open, and I expect it to be Mom, but instead Dad's voice calls out. "Sweet Pea?"

"In here." I sit up and pull a protesting Cheese onto my lap.

"Hey, you know it's Friday, right?"

I nod.

Dad looks around for a minute, and I wonder what it feels like to be back in this house now that he doesn't live

200

here. I'll never forget the first night without him. I kept waking up all night, feeling like I'd forgotten something.

"I just missed Cheese," I say.

And upon hearing his name, Cheese jumps out of my arms and weaves in and out of Dad's legs, purring and letting out the occasional meow. Dad squats down to scratch his chin, and Cheese immediately plops down and rolls over, inviting belly rubs.

"Me too," says Dad. "You don't want to come hang out for a few nights, buddy? Not a fan of split custody, huh?"

Cheese nips lovingly at Dad's knuckle.

It's one small thing, like Kiera said. But I can't stop it. The tears just flow out of me like someone turned on a faucet.

Dad stands up and rushes over to me. "Oh, Sweet Pea. What is it, baby?" He reaches down and pulls me up off my feet and into a hug. And I don't even care that he's still covered in paint from work.

"Nothing," I tell him, my voice cracking. "Everything. Mom has a boyfriend. Oscar's mad at me." And so much more I can't say.

We stand there for a moment in the house that will always belong to all of us as Cheese settles in on top of our feet and Dad lets me cry every tear in my body.

"Let it all out. This isn't easy," Dad says. "This isn't easy for any of us, but especially you. And I'm so, so sorry for that."

I nod, taking a step back as I dry my eyes with the sleeve of my shirt. I'm guessing Mom's boyfriend wasn't news to him.

"You ready to head over to my place?"

"Yeah."

"Oh, hey," says Dad, reaching past me. "My mail! What the heck? How could they send me absolutely nothing and then this?"

He takes the envelope with a red *FINAL NOTICE* stamp across the front and stuffs it into his pocket. I'm tempted to slap it out of his hand—anything I can do to just make time freeze.

As we walk out the door, Cheese surprises us both by following us out to the sidewalk and to Dad's house as we walk hand in hand.

Dad laughs. "This cat calls all the shots, doesn't he?"

CHAPTER TWENTY-SIX

My Calling

On Saturday morning, I wake up before Dad and head on over to Miss Flora Mae's to check the mail for a bundle from Mr. Joe Salazar and to water the plants and play them some Aretha Franklin.

I gasp the moment her voice crackles out of Miss Flora Mae's speakers. I can't believe I hadn't thought of this before! I spent all of last night searching for inspiration for my research project, and the inspiration has been here all along. Aretha Franklin! She is the perfect subject for my research project. Once that decision is squared away, I feel a burden lift from my shoulders, and I'm all ready to skim through the latest stack of letters.

There are all kinds of dilemmas today. There are sibling rivalries, questions about home-brewed cleaning supplies, a woman who's gay and trying to figure out how best to tell her family, parents having trouble communicating with their kids, a scandal involving a recipe thief at the county fair, someone who borrowed money from a friend and can't pay it back, and many, many more. But the letter that strikes me most is all about friendship. And I definitely have an answer.

> Dear Miss Flora Mae,
> Do you ever feel like you can see the end coming? Not the end of the world. I mean, the end of a relationship. I've been through a ton with my best friend, but I've felt like they were pushing me further and further away. At first, I made excuses for them. I thought maybe they were going through a bad time, but these days I can barely remember why our friendship is worth saving. What do I do? Confront them? Break it off? Let fate decide?
> Sincerely,
> High & Dry

I take the letter home with me and send the rest off to Miss Flora Mae.

Monday is basically the best Monday to ever Monday, because it's the last Monday of the school year. No more home-work. And no forced conversation between Kiera and Oscar or awkward stuttering in front of Greg to ruin my day.

When I get home, Mom is rushing around the house and there are hangers everywhere. Not only that, but the ironing board is unfolded in the middle of the kitchen with Cheese sitting on top like we're his royal subjects and all this chaos is his kingdom. And I didn't even know we owned an iron!

"Mom?"

"In here!" she shouts back.

I follow her voice to her bedroom, which is only like half a bedroom, really, because she's left Dad's side totally untouched. Even in all this mess, none of her wardrobe is crossing the invisible boundary dividing his side of the room from hers.

"What are you doing? I thought you didn't get off work for another hour."

She rushes out of her bathroom, her hair half-curled and her robe undone, revealing an old pair of boxer shorts and a grubby old blood-drive T-shirt.

"My last patient canceled. And . . . I've got a date!" she says, her voice raising a few octaves too high.

"Tonight?" Seriously? Why can't we just go back to her dating this guy behind my back?

She twirls around with a light-blue gauze sundress draped over her arm. "Only if you don't mind hanging out with Dad tonight. What do you say? Maybe you can invite a friend over? Oscar or even Kiera?"

"It's—it's a school night," I blurt, like that somehow makes a difference. But it does! What kind of person goes on a date on a school night?

"I don't have to go," she says. And despite the brightness in her voice, her expression tells me she'd be super disappointed.

I feel immediately bad. Mom's always the one who's there to help me through the tough stuff. I once heard her and Dad arguing over how she was always the "responsible" one. If I think about it, that makes a lot of sense, and Mom deserves to let loose too. I guess.

"I'll hang out with Dad," I tell her, the guilt weighing so deeply on me I'm almost sinking into the floor. "You should wear the blue. It looks really nice."

I go to the kitchen and retrieve King Cheese from his throne on the ironing board and take him to my room.

The letter I'd planned on replying to sits on my desk, but I just can't imagine even thinking about someone else's problems right now.

I get into bed and pull the covers up to my chin while

Cheese paws at the door, anxious to get back to his perch, I'm sure. "Come on, buddy. Don't you feel sorry for me?"

He meows in response and nudges the door with his head.

I throw the covers back and let him out before sitting down in front of my desk. I should've just responded to this letter when I had the chance yesterday and when I could use Miss Flora Mae's typewriter. Maybe I'll just throw it away. No one would ever know, especially with all those letters she never responds to. Mine included.

But then I think about the summer after Kiera ditched me. Outside of whatever the heck I'm going through right now with Mom and Dad, it was the loneliest, most confusing time in my life that I can remember. I mean, I'm sure grown adults trying to talk gibberish at me when I was a baby was also confusing, but luckily, I have no memory of that.

My pen hovers above my notepad.

Dear High & Dry,

First things first. No one deserves to be treated the way your friend is treating you. What might be hard to remember is that this probably isn't your fault. I think people are a little bit like boomerangs, and you've got to let them go so that they can come back to you. But also, sometimes people are just bad people and you gotta cut them loose. I don't know what's caused the change in your friend's attitude, but it sounds like something they've got to deal with on their own. So give 'em a taste of their own medicine. If they're ignoring you, how about you ignore them back? And then, when all this blows over, you'll either be down a friend—even if it's a pretty crummy friend—or they'll find their way back to you. But all you can do is live your life and be there for the people who want you around.

Sincerely,
Miss Flora Mae

I sit back in my chair and examine my handiwork. Without a doubt, my best letter to date. I think I've found my calling.

CHAPTER TWENTY-SEVEN

First-Date Jitters

After some proper begging and promising Mrs. Bryant that Kiera and I will spend the night putting the finishing touches on our end-of-year research projects, Kiera gets to come over for a few hours.

As Mom is walking me over to Dad's house, Mr. Bryant's truck pulls up alongside the sidewalk.

As Kiera gets out, her dad calls to Mom, "Hey there, Liz," he says.

She gives him a short wave but says nothing. It's pretty obvious where her loyalty lies.

"Tell, uh, Andre I said hi," he says.

Kiera and I exchange a look.

"You can tell him yourself," Mom says. Without waiting

for Mr. Bryant to respond, Mom turns to me. "Call me if you need anything, baby." She pushes a wave of hair behind my ear, but it's quick to disobey. She searches my face for something. "Are you sure this is okay?"

I let out a quiet sigh and nod. I think she's more nervous about me than she is her date. I gotta be honest: I'm feeling a little queasy myself.

Mom smiles and looks over my shoulder. "Kiera, it's nice to see you back around."

Inside, Dad is cooking up a storm, working on a new recipe he found online that he's been perfecting on his solo nights—ginger-lime chicken with coconut sticky rice.

As the three of us sit around the table, Kiera shovels a spoonful of rice in her mouth and says, "Mr. DiMarco, I never knew rice could be this sweet and salty at the same time."

Dad's mouth spreads into a slow satisfied grin. "Well, I'm honored to have shown you the light, Kiera."

After dinner, Kiera and I sit by the window in my bedroom with the lights off, waiting for Mom's date to pick her up.

"Do we actually have to sit here in the dark?" Kiera asks. "It doesn't matter if she sees us."

"Oh, it totally matters," I tell her. "She can't know that I care."

"That makes absolutely zero sense."

A red truck pulls up outside of Mom's house, and a guy with dark hair parted neatly down the side hops out. He wears crisp-looking jeans and a button-down shirt.

"Oh, he's good," says Kiera. "He's got flowers."

Bunched in his fist is a huge bouquet of bright sunflowers. I gotta admit, they look pretty cheery.

Behind us, my bedroom door swings open and Dad flips the light on. "Dad! Privacy, please!"

"Privacy?" he scoffs. "You're snooping on your mother and you're lecturing me on privacy?"

"Aren't you just a little teensy bit curious?" I ask him.

He steps out of the door frame and motions for Kiera and me to follow him out into the hall. "How 'bout you two work out here in the living room for a while?"

I hold my fingers up in a pinch. "Just a little bit curious?"

Dad rolls his eyes. "Back away from the window."

I throw my hands up and stomp out into the living room with Kiera close behind. "What's the point of us all living on the same street if I can't snoop on you two?"

Kiera and I spend the rest of the night in the living room, working on our projects. Kiera's super organized and has color-coded note cards and glitter glue framing each picture on her poster board of Jungkook and his K-pop band, BTS.

"Quite the operation you've got going on, Kiera," says Dad.

"I take my K-pop bands and schoolwork equally serious," she says in a stern voice.

"Who'd you choose for your project, Sweet Pea?" He thumbs through the pictures Mom helped me print out. "Aretha, huh? She's a classic. A little before your time. I'm surprised you've heard of her."

I feel a little self-conscious, like maybe I should have picked someone else that I know a little more about. "Like you said, she's a classic."

We work on our projects for a little while longer, and I try to show Kiera *America's Most Haunted*, but she's not as into it as Oscar and I are, so we settle on the latest episode of some reality show about little girls in beauty pageants.

After a few hours, Mom's still not home, but it's time for Kiera to go. The three of us pile up in Dad's truck and drive to the edge of town, where the newest houses in Valentine are. Even though it's just Kiera and her parents, they live in a five-bedroom with a pool that Dad always called a McMansion.

As Kiera's hopping out of the truck, her dad opens the front door, and I can feel my dad tense beside me.

It's so weird to see Dad be nervous about anything or anyone.

Mr. Bryant coughs into his fist as Kiera runs through

the doorway and past him. He stands there for a moment before saying, "Thanks, Andre, for uh, dropping her off."

Dad nods. "Not a problem."

And that's it. I almost want to scream at Mr. Bryant to come over here and just talk to Dad. He's the same person he was last year or the year before. Right?

But still, just those few words between them makes something in Dad's posture ease as we drive home under the glow of stars.

CHAPTER TWENTY-EIGHT

Home Sweet Home

At breakfast on Tuesday morning, Mom's sunflowers are on full display. Ever since last night, Mom and Dad are both buzzier than normal, and their vibes are pretty contagious.

I guess that's why there's an extra bounce in my step as I stop at Miss Flora Mae's mailbox to drop off the package of letters for Mr. Joe, including my own letter, which I typed up on the typewriter early this morning.

Just as I'm shutting the door of the mailbox, a dusty black car turns down the street and into the driveway beside me, making a clunking noise as it bottoms out.

She's back. Miss Flora Mae is home. I wonder if she'd notice if I ran inside to make sure her house is just as she left it. And then part of me is sad. Over the last few weeks when neither of my homes felt like home, I found a place with Bette Davis the cat, the radio, and Miss Flora Mae's plants.

I follow the car up the driveway and watch as she pulls into her garage. She swings the car door open, and one bare foot steps out. Mom drives barefoot on long road trips too. Miss Flora Mae groans as she pulls herself out of her car. She wears a long black muumuu and her big cat-eye sunglasses.

"I'd hoped to catch you before you ran off to that school," she calls down the driveway.

I feel like she can see straight through me. "Hi, Miss Flora Mae. How was your trip?"

"Well, I drove overnight, because I just hate exposing my skin to the sun. It'll kill you if you're not careful. My sister's recovering just fine. Stubborn as hell and won't listen to a speck of reason, but she'll be fine."

"That's nice," I say. "I put this week's letters for Mr. Joe in your mailbox, so you should be all set."

"And the plants?" she asks.

"Green as ever," I promise. "Aretha Franklin is pretty awesome, by the way."

"Well, she's more than pretty awesome, I'd say." The word *awesome* sounds like a foreign language coming from her. "Did you have any other problems? Anything I should know about the paper?"

I should tell her. Maybe she wouldn't even be mad. Except that Miss Flora Mae is the most particular person I know, and I can't imagine how much she would blow up if she knew that some nosy thirteen-year-old had stolen letters from her and then answered them herself. I hadn't thought this far ahead to what I might tell her. I guess I just thought I never would have to. I just keep telling myself that she probably doesn't read her own column once it's printed. Why would she need to?

The letter I just stuck in the mailbox is practically screaming in my ear. But I can't take it out of there without her knowing.

"Well?" she asks.

"Everything was great! Not a single problem. All good!" I've got to get out of here. This woman's the kind of person who can see through every white lie.

She takes her sunglasses off and stares me down until I feel like I'm pinned in place and I couldn't move even if I tried.

"Good," she finally says. "Very good."

She reaches into her car and digs into the center console. She takes my hand and presses a cold metal thing into my palm.

I look down to find an old, heavy-feeling brooch. It's a green pod of peas.

"Sweet peas," she says. "Well, put it on ya."

216

I fidget with the pin, and eventually she reaches over and secures it onto my shirt for me.

"For all your trouble. Sweet peas for Sweet Pea."

I look down. Of course, money would have been awesome, but I didn't exactly do my job just as she instructed, and I can't help feeling a little bit guilty. "I thought you didn't like my nickname."

She digs into her pocket and hands me a fistful of five-dollar bills, a couple of singles, and two Susan B. Anthony coins. "Here. I guess this is what you're really wanting." She pats my shoulder and heads past me and into her house. "It's growing on me," she says. "The nickname, I mean."

We spent all day yesterday reviewing for our final exams. When someone complains that we've never had this much work at the end of the school year, Mrs. Young says, "Well, you've never been mere days from entering eighth grade either. The workload is about to change, y'all, and if I don't prepare you for that, I've failed as your teacher."

On Wednesday we finish up our reviews for Thursday's finals, and then we have field day on Friday, our last day. But first we have to survive research presentations. We're so close to summer I can nearly taste the chlorine water of the community pool. I get giddy every time I remember that Kiera has her very own pool and we're actually friends again, so maybe I'll even get to use it.

Just as we break for lunch on Wednesday, I find my way over to Oscar's desk. "Hey, how'd you do on that grammar review?"

He walks past me to where our cubbies are on the side of the room and grabs his backpack. "Fine, I guess."

I eye the contents of his locker to see if maybe he brought his lunch, but he slams the door before I can see. "Aren't you going to lunch?" I ask.

He shakes his head. "I signed up for JV wrestling and my mom is taking me for the physical during lunch."

"Wrestling?" I remember his mom mentioning something on the phone a while ago, but I forgot to ask him about it again. "You don't even like horsing around with your brothers."

"Maybe I do," he says, defiant. "Maybe you don't know everything about me."

His voice is louder and more defensive than I'm used to. Almost like we're . . . fighting. "Well, okay? But I feel like I know a whole lot. I am your best friend, ya know."

He brushes past me. "I gotta go, so I can make it back in time for class."

"We're so behind on *America's Most Haunted* episodes that I've resorted to rewatching the ones we've already seen." He doesn't say anything, so I quickly explain, "I wouldn't watch any of the newer ones without you. Obviously." Oscar and I have a very serious unspoken promise when it comes to *America's Most Haunted*, and we've watched every single episode for the first time together. It's honestly made it easier to not just gobble up the whole thing in one month. Watching an episode without him for the first time would be a betrayal of the highest sort.

All he manages to say is, "Cool."

"I'll see you later!" I call after him. "Good luck with the physical!"

In the cafeteria, I catch up to Kiera and slide onto the bench beside her. "Oscar signed up for JV wrestling."

"I've been thinking about it too!" says Greg from across the table. "Honestly though, I can't wrestle with my glasses, and contacts make my eyes water too much."

I try to smile, but I must be doing a crummy job, because his face falls a little.

"I bet there's some kind of solution for that. Like prescription goggles or something," I say, with forced cheer, and turn back to Kiera, my voice more hushed. "Oscar doesn't even like when his brothers want to wrestle. Or even, like, sweating in general. What's the deal?"

"Maybe he does like doing that stuff." She shrugs. "I don't know. Boys are weird, especially about stuff that's supposed to be manly."

"Why does it have to be like that? Why does it have to be boys versus girls? Or boys do things like wrestling and girls don't? I really don't think Oscar even wanted to sign up. It's like he just wants to do anything that doesn't involve me."

Kiera shakes her head. "I doubt that's it."

But I can hear the hesitation in her voice, and I know that I'm not entirely wrong.

Later that day, after school, I try to find Oscar to invite him over, but he's already gone.

CHAPTER TWENTY-NINE

Causing a Scene

I spend Wednesday night putting the final touches on my Aretha Franklin project. I read just the other day that she released her first album when she was only fourteen years old. That's only one year older than me, and I can barely get it together enough to finish this project on time. Forget an album.

By Thursday morning, I'm—well, I won't say I'm ready, but I will say that if I don't get this presentation over with today, I might just explode.

As soon as we're done with our pledges and moment of reflection, Mrs. Young asks if there are any volunteers who would like to get their presentations over and done with.

My hand shoots up in the air along with Kiera's, but I guess I beat her to it, because I'm the first to go.

My sweaty hands grip the edges of my poster board, and I could kiss my mother for having the genius idea of gluing my note cards on the back. Maybe she does have some good ideas.

I clear my throat. "I decided to do my project on Aretha Franklin, the Queen of Soul. She was a singer, songwriter, pianist, actress, and civil-rights architect." No, that's not right. "Activist, I mean. A civil-rights activist."

Someone sniggers. I think. Somewhere on the far side of the classroom. Or maybe it's just in my head. I feel like my skin is on fire and like everyone can see my underwear, which are days-of-the-week underwear, and I think I'm accidentally wearing my Sunday pair.

Mrs. Young said to be sure to look up and make eye contact, but I can't bring myself to do it and instead just power through all the facts I learned about Aretha's early life. "And when Aretha left Columbus—I mean Columbia Records—for Atlantis . . . I'm sorry, Atlantic Records, she gained more control over her career and her sound."

Another laugh starts a low ripple through the classroom, but this time I know that laugh. I look up to see Oscar—my Oscar!—laughing as he leans over and whispers something to Alyssa that makes her laugh even harder.

They're clearly making fun of me. My eyes dart over to Kiera and she gives me a subtle thumbs-up.

"Ms. Franklin's famous song, 'Respect,' became an anthem for the civil-rights movement. And—and . . ." I take a deep breath, but Oscar's laugh echoes in my ears, and I can't seem to find my place again.

"Take your time, Sweet Pea," says Mrs. Young gently. "You're doing fine."

Her interference brings on another quiet buzz of conversation among my classmates.

I nod. "When Aretha sang at Dr. Martin Luther King Jr.'s memorial, her voice was a light in a very dark time. And that is still true to this day." I glance over to Mrs. Young with her bright-orange lipstick and watermelon-print dress. She spares me a wink. "Even for me," I add, more quietly.

I train my eyes on the rest of my presentation and force myself not to stray even if it means losing points for eye contact. I can't believe I volunteered to go first. What was I thinking? Probably the same thing I was thinking when I thought it'd be a good idea to answer Miss Flora Mae's letters.

I finish my presentation and the whole class claps, but only because Mrs. Young has made it clear that clapping for everyone is part of our participation grade.

"You did good," Kiera whispers as I sit down. I know that's not entirely true and that she's just being nice, but hearing her say so makes me feel a tiny bit better anyway.

Kiera stands up with her beautiful and extremely professional trifold poster board about Mae Jemison, the first African American woman in space. Apparently, her mother wasn't as excited about her K-pop star idea as Kiera was. Regardless, Kiera is a pro. Heck, she doesn't even need to use her note cards. She's as good at speaking in front of all of us as Mrs. Young is.

I think about how nervous I was up there and how I stumbled over my words and how much it made me feel better to see Kiera out there giving me the thumbs-up, so I try to keep eye contact while she is talking. I just can't believe Oscar talked through my whole presentation and didn't even laugh at my jokes. He knows there's nothing worse than making a joke that doesn't land. Talk about awkward. Even worse was that he laughed at the parts that weren't even supposed to be funny! My chin begins to quiver as the tears threaten to spill. I bite down hard on my lip to keep it together.

Kiera finishes and gives a quick curtsy, and the whole class claps *and* cheers! They cheer! If we weren't friends again, I might just hate her.

Before lunch, Mrs. Young holds up a clipboard. "I've got field day sign-ups all ready to go. Partner up with a friend and write it down up here. Since we're an odd number this year, I'll be partnering up with whoever doesn't find someone else in time. And to be totally honest, whoever ends up with me is in luck, because I'm one half of the winning team at the Young Family Reunion—three years running!"

I turn around to tell Kiera I should partner up with Oscar, but she beats me to it.

"You should sign up with Oscar," she says. "Maybe it will give y'all a chance to get over whatever his problem is."

"Are you sure?" I ask.

Greg saunters up the row behind us. "Y'all partnering up?" he asks. "Coop says our height ratio is no good for the three-legged race."

"I think this is probably the first time he's let you out of his sight since you moved here," says Kiera with a snicker.

Greg laughs nervously. "Coop is, uh, a good friend."

"Actually," I say, "I think I'm with Oscar, but you and Kiera should sign up together."

Greg shrugs and nods.

Kiera does the same. "Sold."

Besides if I had to partner up with Greg, I don't think I could trust myself to even walk in a straight line properly.

After waiting my turn with the clipboard, I see that Oscar is already signed up, so I go to fill in the blank next to his name with mine.

But he's already signed up. With Alyssa.

WHAT. THE. HECK?

Now I'm just mad. I speed walk all the way to the cafeteria where Oscar sits—not even at our usual table—with Alyssa and her posse of Samantha and Tyler.

I throw my hands up. "What's your problem with me?" I ask.

The entire fifth- and sixth-grade classes pause as they file into the cafeteria, and I can sense Kiera approaching from the side, but her expression says it all: she's too late.

Oscar takes a bite out of his sandwich. "I don't know what you're talking about."

"You won't take my phone calls and you're doing all kinds of stuff without even talking to me about it first and then you're ignoring me and now you've signed up for field day without me!" I can feel my voice getting louder and louder and closer to tears. "We've done every field day together for the last three years."

He puts his sandwich down. "Well, you haven't been a very good friend. You ditched me! And for the person who's treated us like dirt, Sweet Pea." He points to Kiera, who crossed her arms defiantly across her chest.

Kiera scoffs behind me.

"If you just got to know her, you'd like her." But I know that Kiera has had plenty of time to make an impression on Oscar. Maybe it's not fair for me to expect him to just suddenly like her overnight. But doesn't he trust me?

"I know her well enough to know she doesn't think highly enough of either of us, but especially you, to treat us anything more than bugs squashed under her toe. And you've been weird lately, okay? Like, running off on all these secret things and not telling me what's going on. That doesn't make me feel very good, and I definitely don't feel trusted."

I open my mouth, but there are no words. Because he's right. I have been sneaking around without any explanation, and my parents' divorce has made me want to slink away into a cave with just me and Cheese. And sometimes Kiera, because she at least understands what's going on a little bit.

"I even wrote to Miss Flora Mae, and you wanna know what she said? She said people are like boomerangs, and you've got to let them go so that they can decide if they want to come back to you. She confirmed what I was feeling all along. And guess what? I don't even think I care if we're friends anymore. If you're gonna ignore me, I can do the same right back to you."

The letter. It only ran in the newspaper this morning, but I'd somehow forgotten I'd ever even written it. I didn't even check the paper today. All I could think about was my project. "I didn't know it was *me* you were talking about!" I say. "I never would have responded that way if I knew you'd written the letter."

I clap both my hands over my mouth, but it's too late. Oh crud. My big secret. My big mouth. When I first read that letter, I could so easily understand how the sender felt. Kiera had made me feel that exact same way. I knew that Oscar and I were having a rough time, but it hadn't even occurred to me that I could make him feel just as bad.

"*You* never would've responded?" he asks, his brow furrowed into a knot. But then his eyes widen as it dawns on him. "*You*. You wrote that response from Miss Flora Mae?" He lets out a sharp gasp. "You've been writing her advice column this whole time, haven't you? Is that why you've been sneaking around? I saw you go over to her house in the middle of the night the other week. But why would you do that?" He shakes his head and lowers his voice, but he's still plenty loud for everyone to hear. "Is she dead? Did that old vampire finally die?"

I throw my arms up, exasperated. "No! She's not dead. And I didn't answer all of them. Just a few. That's it. And she's not a vampire! She's . . . eclectic!" I nearly scream the word.

"Sweet Pea?" asks Kiera.

I forgot she was standing right there. I look around and see the faces of the entire lunch period, basically everyone fourth grade and up. They heard me. They all heard me. My throat tightens, and I can't think of a single thing to say. I can't even make myself deny it.

Kiera's voice breaks the silence again. "Is that true? You've been answering Miss Flora Mae's letters? What about . . ."

She doesn't want to say it out loud. I can see that. Everyone would know she'd needed the advice in the first place. She's wide-eyed and caught off guard in a way I've never seen before.

I can hear the whispers rumbling all around. *Miss Flora Mae is Sweet Pea. Sweet Pea killed Miss Flora Mae. She's been lying. She knows everyone's secrets.* Only a few people around us have caught on, but I wonder how long it will take for the whole class to find out.

"Sweet Pea?" I turn to find Mrs. Young. "Let's take this to the office, okay?"

I nod numbly.

I look to Oscar, hoping to find sympathy there, but he won't even look at me. And Kiera . . . she's still shocked, but I can see the hurt building like a wall around her.

I don't know how to fix this. I don't even know where to start.

CHAPTER THIRTY

A New Kind of Normal

In the office waiting area, the word I hear Mrs. Young use over and over when she's on the phone with my mom is *disruptive*. Apparently, I "caused a scene." I was "acting out of character." Mrs. Young wants to know if "something is going on at home." I nearly shout: *Which home?*

Mrs. Young circles back around the front of the receptionist's desk. "Your mother is on her way, Sweet Pea. When she gets here, we'll have a chat with Vice Principal Mendes."

"Am I in trouble?" I ask.

"That's up to Vice Principal Mendes." She gives me a sympathetic half smile. "I've got to get back to the rest of the class, but I'll be back when your mother arrives," she says, and leaves me there in the waiting area outside the offices. It feels more like a holding pen.

About thirty minutes in, and the tears start falling. My mom still isn't here. I think I'm in trouble. Oscar hates me. Kiera probably does too. And I blew my big secret. It's probably only a matter of time before Miss Flora Mae finds out too.

From behind her desk, Miss Horton, the school receptionist, slides a tiny bowl of hard candy toward me. "The red ones are strawberry," she says.

I take one and slump back into my seat. The front office waiting area is just one giant windowed room looking out into the hallway, so I'm basically on display for everyone to see as they file back to class from the cafeteria. I turn my back to avoid having to make eye contact with everyone.

While Miss Horton is in the teachers' lounge microwaving her lunch, Greg pops his head through the cutout in the glass where the attendance slips are dropped off.

"Hey," he whispers.

I twirl around to find the hallway completely empty except for him. The fluttering in my stomach I normally feel around Greg is faint. My mind is full of too many other things to even worry about Greg.

"Just taking a quick bathroom break," he explains.

"Cool." I honestly just don't even want him—or anyone else—to see me right now.

"Are you, uh, okay?"

Do I *look* okay? I feel like when people ask that, they don't really want to know the truth, but I get the feeling Greg is asking to really know.

I grimace a little when I say, "I don't think so."

"Is it true what everyone's saying? About you and those letters?"

Who knows what he's heard about me by now? But at least part of it is true. "Yeah, there's some truth to it."

He shrugs and his whole lanky body flops. "Well, I bet you'd give some pretty good advice. My parents are always reading her column since we got here."

"Thanks," I whisper.

"I better get back to class." He bites down on his lip. "Hey, Sweet Pea?"

"Yeah?"

"I know that things have been, like, weird because of your parents and everything. I get it. Stuff has changed a lot for me this year too." He shrugs again with his whole body.

I think I get what he's trying to say. "Moving must have been pretty hard," I say.

He lets out a low chuckle. "Uh, yeah. Starting at a new school kind of stinks. Even if everyone is pretty cool.

But it's not the same. At my old school me and my friends started a club called Paranormal Appreciation Society. How could I ever find anything that cool again?"

"Everybody here likes you," I tell him. And it's not just because he's the new guy. People really like him. But a Paranormal Appreciation Society does sound pretty epic. I would totally join. Guilt begins to settle in the pit of my stomach as I realize I haven't done much to be Greg's friend, especially when he could probably use one. He just didn't seem like he needed any help, honestly.

"And I like it here too," he says. "It's just different. A new kind of normal, I guess."

We both look up as we hear Miss Horton slam the microwave door shut in the other room.

He smiles. "I'll see you later."

"See ya!" I call after him as he heads off down the hallway back to class.

I think about what Greg said while I wait a little while longer. This whole time I thought it was Mom and Dad who were stuck trying to keep things the way they were, but maybe I'm not so good at change either.

Finally, Mom rushes into the front office breathlessly. Why couldn't they have called Dad?

"I got here as soon as I could," she announces. "I had to move a few clients around." She presses the back of her hand to my forehead. "Are you feeling okay?" She turns to Miss Horton. "So unlike her to have outbursts at school."

I push her hand away. "I'm fine."

Inside Vice Principal Mendes's office, Mom and I sit down, and Mrs. Young stands behind Vice Principal Mendes, a tall woman with chin-length blunt hair. It's not that I don't get into trouble, but I usually don't get caught, so up until now, I've had little reason to tango with VP Mendes.

"It was a very distracting outburst," Mrs. Young explains, her voice riddled with confusion. "She yelled at another student in the middle of the cafeteria. That's really out of character for Sweet Pea."

Why do they have to talk about me like I'm not right stinking here?

Mrs. Young continues. "I just wonder if things at home might be contributing to this kind of behavior." The way she says it isn't mean or judgmental. Just like she actually cares.

Mom looks caught off guard. "Well . . . I—I . . ." She clears her throat. "Sweet Pea's father and I have gone to great lengths to keep this divorce as civil as possible."

Mrs. Young nods.

Vice Principal Mendes leans forward. "Perhaps Sweet Pea doesn't feel like she has space to express herself and her feelings about the divorce, and so she's taking it out on her friends. Publicly."

Mom turns to me. "Is that true, Sweet Pea?"

I don't even know how to answer that. All those words basically sounded like one giant, jumbled-up math equation. "Am I in trouble?"

Mom turns to Mrs. Young for the answer. "Vice Principal Mendes and I discussed it and we think it would be best to send her home for the rest of the day, give her some space to think on her actions. But she's welcome back tomorrow. Luckily, she already did her presentation. She can come in early tomorrow to finish her essay questions and multiple choice."

"But my brain can't even think before eight a.m.!"

All three adults turn to me with a *not our problem* look on their faces. Even Mrs. Young.

"Fine," I mutter.

Mom spends the whole drive home on the phone, rearranging the rest of her day's appointments. As she hangs up from her final call, she pulls into the driveway but doesn't immediately turn the car off.

"Do you want to talk about what happened today, Sweet Pea?"

I shake my head.

"Are you and Oscar fighting?"

I shrug. "It's silly. It's just a misunderstanding." I think about how I did basically tell him to ditch me in my letter to him, so maybe I deserve this.

Mom's phone vibrates where it sits in the cup holder. She picks it up and reads the incoming message, smiling for a moment before realizing, *Oops, I'm supposed to be having a heart-to-heart with my clearly upset daughter.*

I sit up a little higher and take a peek at her phone. *Sam.* Her boyfriend. "Are you serious?" I throw my hands up in the air. "Are you seriously distracted by your boyfriend right now? At this very moment? You're supposed to be the parent!" I remind her.

"Sweet Pea, baby." She goes to put a hand on my knee, but I flinch away.

"Do whatever you want. Call your boyfriend, for all I care. Tell him you love him and want to have a million babies," I say. "I'm going to Dad's."

"But it's not his night," she says, like going over there on any day that doesn't belong to him is somehow as preposterous as rainbow-colored unicorn poop.

"I don't care whose night it is." I grab my backpack and get out of the car, slamming the door behind me before she has a chance to stop me.

I hoof it over to Dad's house, passing Miss Flora Mae where she sits on her screened-in porch. I shake my head. That's a whole problem I can't even think about right now.

I walk right into Dad's house like it's my house because it is. This is my house.

"Dad?" I call.

I hear some kind of muttering and catch Dad sweeping aside some papers as I walk into the kitchen.

"Sweet Pea! You're supposed to be in school!"

I give him a quick recap. "I got in trouble. Mom picked me up. And now she's giggling with her boyfriend while I'm trying to talk to her, and I just can't even look at her right now."

"You got in trouble? Why didn't you call me?"

I shrug. "The school called Mom."

"Well, why didn't she call me?"

My fists clench as I groan. "I don't know. Maybe you should ask her." It's like they want to be a family when things are warm and fuzzy and easy, but what about when things are hard and no one is happy?

One single paper falls loose from his teetering stack on the kitchen table and I get to it before he does.

It's a watercolor painting of a bright-white storefront with a royal-blue sign. The sign reads "DiMarco Hardware and Art Supplies." The windows are painted for fall with pumpkins and falling leaves.

I can feel my chin quivering. I thought if I just ignored this and hid all his mail that this might not happen. That this would just all go away. "What is this?"

"Sweet Pea, sit down."

"Tell me what it is," I demand.

"I need to go back to Connecticut for a little while."

"And you're just now telling me?" I throw my hands up. "Just like you never told me about wanting to be a real painter and all those paintings in your third bedroom."

"That's just some silly hobby." He smiles like he thinks I'm young and silly, and that only makes me angrier.

"One you never shared with me!"

"You're right," he concedes.

"You hid a whole part of yourself from me. I thought we didn't have any secrets."

He chuckles a little like I'm being ridiculous. "Sweet Pea, those paintings are just a thing I do to pass the time. Like I said, just a hobby. I wasn't trying to hide anything from you."

But it feels like he was. Mom had the perfect plan for the perfect identical houses, except Dad's house had a whole extra room for him to keep his secrets.

"And now you're leaving me with *her*. Why can't I come with you?"

Dad shakes his head. "Sweet Pea, it's not like that. I've got some business to take care of. Things I have to do on my own. Your mother and I have talked about this, and we think it's best if you stay down here with your friends."

"I don't have any friends left! Well, good luck in Connecticut," I say, practically spitting the words at his feet. "I'm sure you'll be just fine without me."

I'm gone, slamming another door, racing down the steps and back down the sidewalk.

I pause for a moment in front of Mom's gate. And then I start to walk back to Dad. I double back again.

I can't bear to see either of them right now.

I find myself pacing in front of Miss Flora Mae's house for a few minutes before I finally give in and walk up her walkway. She's not on the porch anymore, so I ring her gilded doorbell—something I've never done. I don't know where she got the thing, but if there's such a thing as a spooky-doorbell store, Miss Flora Mae is probably their best customer.

I ring the bell again.

The door creaks open, and there's Miss Flora Mae in her black muumuu and a giant pair of slippers that look like clawed wolf paws.

"Can I come in?"

She gives me a quizzical look. "Enter at your own risk."

Dear Miss Flora Mae,

I'd be in deep trouble if Mom and Dad knew I was spilling their secret. They haven't even told Grandma or Aunt Cheryl. You probably won't even read this anyway, so what does it matter?

My mom and dad are getting a divorce. I wish there was a way I could stop it. But I can't. No one can. Because my dad is gay, and trying to stop the divorce is like asking him to be someone else. At least that's what my mom said.

I don't even know what I'm trying to ask. All I know is my world is actually splitting in two and I'm being pulled in every direction. We all love each other, but it's like on those shows about doctors where they need a certain kind of blood for a patient, but all they have is the wrong kind. This is what that feels like. We have plenty of love. It's just not the right kind.

Sincerely,
Caught in the Middle

UNANSWERED

CHAPTER THIRTY-ONE

Stuck in the Middle

"I was wondering how long you'd be pacing that ever-loving street before you decided to come inside," says Miss Flora Mae. "I've been gone for three weeks and you've already taken up my spot as town eccentric."

"Eccentric?" I ask.

"Weirdo," she supplies. "They can't get enough of my advice, but just about the whole lot of them think I'm storing bodies in the basement."

"But you don't even have a basement," I say.

"Not that you know of." She winks. "Have a seat on the couch. I'll get us some lemonade." She calls over her shoulder, "Though by the looks of it you much prefer my ginger ale."

Eeek! I wonder what other little differences she noticed around the house. I sit down on the couch, and even though I've gotten quite used to this place, I suddenly feel like a guest.

She returns with two glasses. After handing me one, she sits in the armchair across from me.

I feel my secret about answering some of her letters crawling up my throat. Like I've swallowed a grasshopper and the poor fella survived the whole ordeal, but he's still gotta find his way out.

"You ready to tell me what's the matter?"

"It's my parents," I huff. "And my friends. Particularly my best friend." I almost let it slip that one of the letters I answered for her backfired on me in a major way. "And then there's Kiera, who suddenly wants to be my friend again, but I think I messed that up, and now I'm doubly friendless. Plus this whole business with my parents trying to live practically next door to each other." I keep going, because now that I'm talking, I can't stop. I tell her all about school today and getting in trouble and Oscar joining the wrestling team and Dad getting all these phone calls from a bank in Connecticut and Mom dating, which is still so gross to me.

"Sounds like you got a lot on your mind." The words drawl out slowly as she balances a pencil between her fingers.

A lot on my mind? Uh, yeah. To say the least! "Well, maybe if you'd read the letters I sent you over the last few years, you might have known that." I immediately regret my decision to say that out loud.

"Hmm," is all she says.

I take a huge gulp of lemonade, because I don't know what else to do with this cringeworthy silence.

Finally, Miss Flora Mae asks, "And none of this has anything to do with the letters you answered in my advice column?"

I spit the lemonade back into the glass. "What? What are you talking about?" The moment the words are out of my mouth, I know playing innocent is the wrong move. Miss Flora Mae might be an odd one, but she's smart as a whip.

"Don't you play the fool with me, Sweet Pea."

Something about her using my nickname instead of Patricia makes me a little less anxious. I set the glass back down and am actually kind of sad that I've ruined a perfectly good glass of lemonade. Crossing my arms, I let out a loud *hmph*. "How'd you know?"

"Well, I'd planned on reading the papers when I returned home, but when Mr. Joe emailed me the proofs, I noticed letters I hadn't written. I may be old, but I'm no sucker."

My. Mind. Is. Blown. "You have *email?*" I ask, shocked.

It's like someone's just proved the Earth is actually flat. I can't believe it.

"Dear, I'm all over the interwebs."

"B-but why would you make me do all that busywork sending you your letters when Mr. Joe could have just emailed you?"

"First off, nothing about what you did was busywork. And like I said, I've got a routine."

I shake my head. "But am I in trouble for answering the letters?"

"Not with me, you aren't." She studies the mantel, where Bette Davis sits. "I know I oughta punish you, but sometimes the moments that shape us are a result of a little bit of mischief."

"What about Mr. Joe?"

She chuckles. "He's none the wiser. For a former investigative reporter, he's not all that sharp."

"I didn't mean to do it," I tell her. "The first one was more of an accident. But then I liked it. I liked helping people and looking for a way to fix their problems."

She lets a small grin slide. "You've got the bug. And I'll admit: you weren't all that bad at answering. But it sounds like the letters might have gotten the best of you."

I nod. "Well, the first letter fixed things with Kiera, but then with Oscar—it just made a huge mess."

She gives me a rigid smile, the kind my mom does when she's got news that's bad for me but maybe not for her. It feels like that's been happening with me and adults a whole lot lately.

"Sweet Pea," Miss Flora Mae says, "I've got to wonder . . ." She pauses a moment, and I wait for the other shoe to drop. The bad news to balance out her good news. "Maybe Oscar isn't the problem. Or your dad or your mom."

"What's that supposed to mean?" I can't help but feel defensive.

"What that means is that maybe you weren't being the best friend to Oscar and maybe your mother *should* date if she wants to. She's a grown woman after all."

"But it's so soon. And everything's happening so fast. . . ."

She sets her glass on the coffee table and leans forward. "I know seeing your parents move on from each other must be painful, but that doesn't mean they're leaving you behind."

"Everything was fine before Dad . . . well . . ."

"Before your father announced he was gay."

I nod. Of course she knows.

Miss Flora Mae gives me a good long look before saying, "Maybe it was fine for you, but trust me when I tell you, my dear, that if your parents don't take care of themselves, they can't take care of you. Have you ever been on an airplane?"

"Three times," I tell her. And all three times were to go to Connecticut.

"Good," she says. "Do you remember the flight attendant telling the passengers that should the air masks release from above that the adults should put their masks on before helping those around them?"

I nod.

"And did you ever feel like that sounded a teensy bit selfish?"

"Well, now that I think about it, yeah."

She leans forward toward me. "That's because your parents can't help you breathe if they can't breathe for themselves. You understand?" Leaning back, she rests her arms on her armchair, like it's a throne. "I don't have all the answers, despite what my advice column might lead you to believe, but there's more to marriage than being a parent, and there is oh so much more to being a parent than being married."

There's just one thing I can't manage to understand. "But why does Dad have to leave? Why would he do that?"

"That's not for me to answer. But I'll tell you one thing: he can't answer if you won't listen. Stomping back and forth down the street doesn't look like you've given him much of a chance if you ask me. Talk to him."

"Can I ask you another question?"

"Shoot."

"What about my letters?" I ask. "The ones I've sent you. How come you never responded?"

She stands up, stretching so hard a few bones creak and pop.

All at once I feel very foolish. Of course she doesn't have time to answer every single letter.

I watch as she walks into the kitchen and opens the oven, where she keeps her important papers, digging around for a minute until she comes up with a beige folder. She walks back over to where I'm sitting in the living room and drops the folder on my lap. Written on the tab in a gentle cursive, it says, *The Sweet Pea Files*.

I open the folder and there they are. Each letter I've written to Miss Flora Mae. A rush of embarrassment makes me clam up, and I think I'd rather just take these letters and bury them in my backyard next to my pet hamster, Sir Waffles (RIP, Sir Waffles).

"So I guess you don't respond to every letter?"

She sighs. "Well, there are two answers to that question. The first is: kid, I get a lot of letters. There aren't enough hours in a day to answer 'em all. For a town this small, there are certainly a lot of people looking for a user's manual to this thing called life. And, ya know, to be perfectly honest, if you just read my responses and think for a

247

little while, I bet you could find that I've already answered all your questions. It's just that someone else was doing the asking."

"And what's your other answer?"

She smirks. "My second answer is that sometimes you've just gotta live through life without any shortcuts. Sometimes the only way you can figure out which way is up is to swim to the surface all on your own. It stinks, but it's true. And sometimes people answer their own questions in their letters. Writing can help suss things out, but sometimes we don't see the answer because it's not the one we'd hoped for."

I sigh so hard my lips sound like a motorboat. That's what Mom would call some hard truth. But I bet it's true for everyone. Even Mrs. Young or Cliff VanWarren or Miss Flora Mae herself.

"So that's why you didn't respond to my letters?"

"Mostly," she says. "Plus, I knew they were from you, and I don't have any kind of code of ethics for advice columnists, but something about responding to people I know when I have more details about them than their letters lets on feels like cheating."

"But you still kept them?"

She chuckles. "I didn't say I wasn't tempted to respond."

"Well, then help me now. Please? What do I do about Oscar?"

She coughs up a dry laugh. "Well, I find that when I'm having trouble expressing myself, it helps if I try writing a letter."

"All the kids at school know," I say. "Or at least they're about to. They know I answered some of your letters. A few even think I killed you and took over your job entirely." I shouldn't say it, but I'm going to anyway. "You know some kids even think you're a vampire."

"The only vampire I'm related to is Count Chocula." She waves her hand, brushing away the gossip. "Let 'em think what they want. You've got a knack for this, my dear, and I don't serve up compliments for fun. But first you've got to sort things out with your parents and this Oscar boy. I won't have all this pacing back and forth in front of my house. It'll stress my plants out."

I feel awful about Oscar, and I hate that I pushed him so far away. "You think a letter might do the trick?"

She leans back in her armchair. "Not just any letter."

CHAPTER THIRTY-TWO

Three Legs Are Better Than Two

Mrs. Young bends down to tie my ankle to hers. "Too tight?" she asks. Her hair is in two huge buns on either side of her head. She wears big yellow sunglasses with lenses that look like lemons and a T-shirt that says *Texas Derby Divas* with a pair of roller skates on the front.

I tug on the rope a little. "Nope."

"You feeling any better?" she asks more quietly.

For the first time a heavy weight sinks in my chest, and I realize that I'm really going to miss Mrs. Young. "Well, waking up extra early for my test wasn't great, but at least we didn't finish last in the wheelbarrow race."

She holds her hand up for a high five. "Told you I've got skills."

And she wasn't wrong. Maybe teachers aren't an alien species after all. Actually, I take that back. Teachers are total aliens from another galaxy, but at least most of them come in peace.

Since I stormed off before I had a chance to sign up with anyone else yesterday, I was the lucky one to end up with Mrs. Young. I wasn't exactly pumped about spending my last day of seventh grade tied to my teacher, but I guess there are worse things. Like spiders. And toilet paper stuck to your shoe. And oatmeal-raisin cookies where the raisins look like chocolate chips.

Greg and Kiera are partnered up at the end. I'm sure Kiera's mad at me, but I'm hoping she'll understand I didn't mean to hurt her. Still, I'm nervous to even see her. We were only just getting back on track again. And Oscar . . . Oscar won't even look at me. I've got a plan, though.

Last night, I left Miss Flora Mae's and went back to Mom's, where she and Dad were sitting on the steps to the front porch just like old times.

The two of them scooted apart and made room for me in between them.

"I guess we have to talk," I said.

They both draped an arm over my shoulder and Dad said, "How about you let me do some talking first? Fair?"

"Fair."

"Sounds fair to me," Mom said.

"Sweet Pea," Dad said, "I'm not moving for good. But I am going back up to Connecticut for the summer."

"For what?" I asked.

He glanced over my head to Mom and she gave him a nod. "Grandma's not doing so hot. She's got dementia."

That sounded like some kind of awful dementor rock band from Harry Potter. "What's that mean?"

Mom's voice was gentle as she said, "It means her brain isn't what it used to be and that she can't take care of herself like how she always has. She'll also have a hard time with her memory and always knowing where she is and when it is."

"But . . ." My voice cracked a little bit as I tried not to cry. "Will she remember who I am?" I didn't know Grandma as well as I knew Nana, my mom's mother, but what I did know about Grandma was that she was bossy and didn't take nonsense from anyone. I can't imagine her ever needing help taking care of herself . . . and I felt bad for Dad too. The last few months with my parents had been a lot, but I couldn't imagine what I'd do if that ever happened to one of them.

"Sometimes," said Dad. "And other times, she won't." His mouth pressed together in a thin line, and I could see this was hard for him to talk about.

"But what about all the mail you've been getting? And I heard a voice mail about a loan to open a business?"

"Well, that's the good news," said Dad. "When I get home, I'm buying Love's Hardware."

"What? No way!" I wiped away the stray tear that had escaped.

His lips split into an uncontainable grin. "And I'll be selling art supplies too."

"Will you still be painting?" I asked.

"I'll do window paintings still, like for Honey's Diner or the bank and for the car dealerships around town. And I think I'm going to pick back up again with my bowling league when I get back from Connecticut, so maybe you could come with me and hang out at the arcade like old times."

"But what about, um, Mr. Bryant?"

Dad gave me a look. "I guess you would've heard about that." He nodded. "Sometimes when someone has seen the whole world one way their entire lives, it's hard for them to come around to different ideas. Especially when the people they think they know best aren't exactly who they expected."

"So did Mr. Bryant apologize?" I asked.

"He did in his own way," Dad said. "He's got some things going on in his own life right now and I think he just needed time to adjust."

"I know about him and Mrs. Bryant."

Dad looked over my head to Mom and then back to me

before saying, "You know, part of it is that Mr. Bryant has never really known a gay person as a close friend, and part of it was that seeing me and your mom get a divorce while he's having a hard time with his marriage hit pretty close to home."

I could understand that, but I still felt sick for Kiera.

"But Sweet Pea," said Mom, "all of this means your dad will be moving into the apartment above the hardware store."

I turned to Dad. "You won't live next door anymore?"

He shook his head. "Is that okay with you?"

I didn't realize that in the most unexpected way I'd become attached to the fact that I could just walk a few steps to either of my parents' houses at any given moment. I nodded. "Having the two houses and you both on the same street . . . it felt like a Band-Aid. I want things to be the way they were, but we can't move on if we're stuck in the past."

My parents beamed, like I'd just won first place or landed the leading role in the school play or hit the honor roll.

"It's a shame we can't take all the credit for how smart you are," said Mom.

Dad laughed. "Speak for yourself."

Mom turned to me. "We wanted to give you the best experience possible by living on the same street and even re-creating your room. But maybe that's not giving you the best. Maybe giving you the best means us trying to be our best in our own ways."

Dad nodded. "Life with just Mom and life with just me will never be the same, and it's our fault for trying to force that."

"I don't know what things are going to be like after this, but I think I'm ready as long as it means we're in it together."

Both my parents gripped me in a hug, and I didn't care how tight they were squeezing or that it was too hot outside or that loving their hugs made me feel like a little kid. I just held on to that moment as tightly as they were holding on to me.

Cheese opened the screen door with his forehead and sat on top of my feet, swatting at the occasional firefly as we watched the streetlights come on and the sun dip down behind the houses. The only noise was the occasional laughter or muffled television from a neighboring house.

After a while, Dad went back to his house, and Mom and I went inside. It wasn't the perfect night or anything like that, but it was the most okay I'd felt in a long time. Sometimes it's easy to forget that quiet moments mean just as much as the loud ones, because it's not always about moving. Sometimes it's about sitting perfectly and quietly still.

Mrs. Young and I come in second for the three-legged race. We don't place in any other events, but we don't lose either, and I've got to think that's some kind of win.

Before the start of the big water fight to end the day, I wait in line for frozen watermelon and orange slices while Kiera and Greg squeeze in behind me.

I stand there for a moment, letting all the possible things I should say run through my head, my nerves eating me up.

But then Kiera interrupts me mid-thought by tapping on my shoulder. "I'm not mad." She says it so bluntly that she might as well add in a *duh* at the end. "I know you're overthinking what you should say to me in that head of yours."

I turn around and find that Greg jumped back a few spots to talk to Cooper. He waves, and then turns back to listen intently to Cooper discussing the pros and cons of water guns versus water balloons.

"But you could have told me," she adds.

Relief floods my chest. I nod. "I almost did. That time you spent the night."

"It was smart. What you said. It really made a difference. At least for me it did. My parents are still at each other's throats, but who knows when that will end?"

"It did make a difference? Really?"

"Yeah," she says. "In fact, after you left yesterday, I told everyone that you give just as good advice as Miss Flora Mae. Maybe even better. That shut 'em all up real fast."

What alternate reality is this? "Wow. Thanks for standing up for me, Kiera."

"I wasn't standing up for you. I was just telling the truth."

We make our way to the front and load up with fruit.

Kiera bites down into an orange and holds it in her teeth to give me a huge orange-peel grin. Orange juice runs down her chin, and she doesn't care about being pretty or grown-up.

"Very mature," I tell her. "Very eighth grade of you."

"I'm still a little mad at you," she admits. "You could've just told me the truth." She pushes my shoulder playfully, but I can tell she means it and that I really did hurt her by keeping this from her.

"I'm sorry," I say. "I didn't want to mess things up just as we were figuring things out between us again. I guess I figured it wouldn't do any harm if I didn't tell you."

"But it did. It made me wonder if I could even trust you."

"Then why did you stand up for me?"

"Well, just because you didn't tell me it was you giving advice doesn't mean it wasn't good advice."

"I want you to feel like you can trust me," I tell her.

I don't know how to say it out loud, but hearing that she stood up for me so fiercely makes me want to be an even better friend.

"I want that too." She eats the orange slice and tosses the peel in a trash can. "I think we're gonna be okay, Sweet Pea. Even when we're not."

CHAPTER THIRTY-THREE

Project BFF

Immediately after school, I go over to Miss Flora Mae's house. We spend the afternoon on her screened-in porch with fans buzzing at us from all sides. She answers letter after letter while I face down my last, and hardest, assignment as a seventh grader: Project BFF.

I'm armed with a notepad and pencil, but my brain can't form a thought. All my words are mushed together in my head like one giant pile of melted gummy worms.

I lie there on the floor beneath the slowly whirring ceiling fan. When it's this hot, what's the point of even having fans? All they do is push hot air around. "Miss Flora Mae, can I ask you a question?"

She swivels in her chair to face me and slides her glasses down her nose, lowering her gaze. "Let's hear it."

"Why did you get Bette Davis stuffed after she died? Doesn't it just make you even more sad to be constantly reminded that she's not here?"

"That cat." She chuckles. "That cat *hated* me, but outside of myself, she was the love of my dear husband's life. So he's actually the one who got her stuffed." She pulls up her sleeve to reveal a long scar across her forearm. "You see this thing? This was her parting gift the last time I gave her a flea bath."

I've got a few battle scars from Cheese too. Bette Davis looked like a pretty tough cat, but it sounds like she really belonged to Miss Flora Mae's husband. "But why do you keep her when your husband . . ."

"When he's dead too?" She shrugs and leans back in her chair. "Sometimes it's important to do things for the people you love even when those things don't make a lick of sense to you." She shakes her head. "I hated that dang cat, but I loved her, too, because he loved her."

Bette Davis makes me think of my mom and Sam and my dad and his new business. I want to be excited about the things they're excited about, but it's hard when you feel like you're the past and they're looking toward the future. It also makes me think of Oscar and how things might change between us with Kiera back in my life and him signing up for wrestling and maybe making new friends. But I can't imagine any version of Oscar I wouldn't want in my life.

I stand up and grab the handle on Miss Flora Mae's desk drawer. "May I?"

"Be my guest."

I open the drawer and fish out the red cat-eye glasses without lenses and put them on like I'm suiting up for battle. "Okay if I turn on some music?"

"Please," she says.

I skip back to the plant room and turn up the radio all the way.

Back on the screened-in porch, Miss Flora Mae says, "Oh, yes! The Isley Brothers!"

I bob my head to the music and lie down on my stomach to study the blank pages of my notepad before closing my eyes to let my thoughts slowly begin to thaw into something I can express into words. The Isley Brothers swirl in my head, singing about loving the one you're with, and I think this scheme might take more than a letter.

That night, me, Mom, and Dad all have pizza at Mom's house. We talk more about Dad spending the summer in Connecticut and how Grandma will probably move down here and live with him in his new apartment.

Cheese purrs at my feet, head butting against my shins, in the hopes that he'll get a scrap of pepperoni.

The three of us finish the entire pizza, and Dad even hangs out for a little while and Mom doesn't complain when Dad and I flip the channel over to *Ghostbusters*.

I know there won't be many more times when it's just the three of us, and I know my world is about to get bigger in every way—Mom dating, Dad moving, and me starting eighth grade—but maybe part of growing up means letting people and places change so you can find new ways to love them.

CHAPTER THIRTY-FOUR

Lip-Synching for My Life

I sit on the porch Tuesday morning, waiting for the paper to be delivered. I'm all nerves like I have been the past few weeks, but this time there's a new determination in the air. The moment it lands at my feet, I hop on my bike and tuck it under my arm.

Oscar's house is only a ten-minute bike ride away, but I make it in seven.

I run up the steps to the front door and ring the bell twice.

When no one answers, I try again.

Eventually Jorge stumbles to the door in his sleep shorts.

He doesn't even let me get a word in before he shouts,

"Oscar, Sweet Carrots or whatever you call her is here to see you!"

"It's Sweet Pea," I mutter, but he's already going back to bed. "I know you know my name!" I shout.

High schoolers! So rude!

After a few minutes, Oscar appears at the door wearing a Valentine Junior Varsity Wrestling Team T-shirt.

"Nice shirt," I say.

He crosses his arms. So not amused. "What do you want, Sweet Pea?"

"I have a special delivery for you."

"I have to get to practice."

I hold the paper out for him.

"My mom doesn't subscribe to the paper."

"Well, consider it a gift." I'm not good at hiding the desperation in my voice.

"I'm good," he says and steps past me with a duffel bag slung over his shoulder. "I gotta go."

I watch him walk down the block toward the secondary school and nearly chase him myself, but then I remember: I have a plan B.

I sit down on the walkway leading to his front porch and I open my backpack to do an inventory of my rations. Two bottles of water, a bag of trail mix, one apple, one orange, one baseball hat, sunscreen, and a small My Little Pony karaoke machine from my seventh birthday.

I tug on my baseball hat and liberally apply sunscreen, including the blue zinc oxide that Mom bought me after my nose burned so bad it peeled last summer. Miss Flora Mae would be proud.

I sit and wait. I may not have the best comebacks, and maybe I overthink things to a fault, but one thing I've learned from being the daughter of a therapist is the art of waiting. Before I was allowed to stay home by myself, I spent hours in Mom's waiting room, and at this point, I'm basically a professional at professionally waiting.

About an hour or so into my Olympic gold–worthy session of sitting and waiting, Luis comes out with the lawn mower and doesn't even do a double take when he sees me camped out in his front yard. He just puts his earbuds in and mows the yard as the sun climbs higher and higher into the sky.

There's something soothing about the sound of the mower, and I find myself lying back and using the rolled-up paper as a pillow. And before I know it, I'm nodding off to sleep.

I begin to stir at the sound of approaching footsteps, and I sense a shadow pass over me.

My eyes burn from the sunlight and it takes me a moment to realize Oscar is home and he's just stepped over my lifeless body on his sidewalk.

"Go home, Sweet Pea," he says and slams the door shut

behind him.

Okay. Time to regroup. I fuel myself with an orange, a handful of trail mix, and a bottle of water. I mean business.

I get the karaoke machine out. Time to pull out the big guns. I tested the batteries last night and the volume worked so well that it surprised Cheese and nearly sent him crawling up the wall.

Miss Flora Mae and I curated the perfect playlist. At first, I told her I'd just take the Aretha CD, but she told me that you can't just include Aretha. You have to also include the music that inspired her and the music she inspired.

I hit play on the karaoke machine and Aretha Franklin's "I Say a Little Prayer" begins to play. Miss Flora Mae offered to help me find the version without vocals like a real karaoke machine would play, but I think I could use the real deal for encouragement.

I begin to sing—and let it be known, I'm so bad at singing, my third-grade choir teacher offered to let me be line leader in exchange for not singing too loudly. "The moment I wake up, before I put on my makeup . . . I say a little prayer for you . . ."

After the first verse, a second-story window flies open, and Oscar's middle brother, Jorge, shouts, "Awww, come on! I'm on the phone here!"

"Nope!" I shout back.

"What do I have to do to make you stop?"

The first song ends and the first few notes of Sister Sledge's "We Are Family" begins to play. "Send Oscar down and the singing stops!"

My intention was for Oscar to be so moved by my willingness to embarrass myself in front of his whole block that he would just be forced to forgive me, but if it takes holding his whole family hostage with my horrific vocals, then I'm fine with that too.

"We are family!" I shout-sing into the microphone so loudly that my speakers screech. "Get up everybody and sing!"

The song is nearly over by the time the front door swings open and Oscar steps through the dark doorway.

"All right, all right," he says. "You can turn it off now. My brothers are threatening to make eighth grade a living hell if you don't stop."

I reach down and twist the power dial off. "I brought you the paper," I say.

He plops down beside me. "If you want me to read something in there, you're just gonna have to read it to me yourself."

Suddenly my mouth is dry and my nerves are frazzled. "Sure. Right." I open the paper to the middle and shake it out before clearing my throat. "'Dear Reader, I'm proud to announce the latest addition to my column, *Sweet Pea's Corner*. Sweet Pea is a thirteen-year-old resident of

Valentine, Texas, who will be tackling one letter every time this column runs. I think you'll find her insight to be a welcome addition. And like I've always said, wisdom has no age. And with that, I'll let Sweet Pea introduce herself. Sincerely, Miss Flora Mae.'"

Oscar stands up. "What do you want me to say, Sweet Pea? Good for you? You got your own section in the paper. Big whoop!"

"Will you just wait?" I beg him. "Give me a minute."

He sits back down. "Well, get on with it."

I exhale deeply and then let it all out. "'Dear Readers, Sweet Pea here. First things first: I don't know everything. There have been plenty of times when I thought I did, and those are usually when I've made my biggest mistakes. Mistakes like keeping secrets from the people I love the most and pushing aside the ones who have always been there even when I wasn't worth being there for. I always thought Miss Flora Mae had all the answers, but one thing I've learned from her is that we're all just doing the best we can with the information we have. Sometimes seeing something from a distance or from a different point of view is all it takes to figure out what you should have seen all along. Like my mom says: we all have our blind spots.

"'My blind spot? It made me take my best friend for granted. It had me thinking he'd be there for me no matter what, even when I treated him like cow dung. So today, before I have any letters to answer, I'd like to take this chance to say: Oscar, with the way I've been acting, I'm not worthy of a friend like you, but I'm going to do my best to be the kind of friend who deserves you. I know things are changing between us with lots of new stuff ahead, but the thing I've figured out lately is that change doesn't have to be bad. Change can be an adventure even if it includes eighth grade and JV wrestling. Ready for the Adventure, Sweet Pea.'"

I fold the paper up and set it down between us.

Oscar's quiet for a long minute.

"Well?" I ask.

"Your own corner, huh?" He smiles. "That's some real power."

"I wanted to tell you," I say. "About helping out Miss Flora Mae. But she swore me to secrecy, and I didn't realize keeping other people's secrets would mean keeping so many secrets from you."

His shoulders slump. "I just missed you, is all. And then I thought you were trading me in for Kiera." He shakes his head. "I just didn't get how you could do that after she did the same thing to you."

"She apologized," I offer. "And I want to give her a second chance. But she's no replacement for you. Nobody is."

"You're right about that," he says.

"So you forgive me?" I ask.

"That depends. You promise to never sing in front of my house again?"

"Hey!" I tell him. "Desperate times called for desperate measures."

He throws his arm over my shoulder. "Yeah," he says. "I forgive you."

"You really joined the wrestling team?"

He curls his arm up and flexes. "Turns out I'm pretty great at it. All those years roughhousing with my brothers paid off. And they really need someone in my weight class."

"Do you like it?" I ask.

"Yeah." He sounds like he's surprising even himself. "I really do. Sometimes my brain is spinning so fast I can't keep up, but when I'm on the wrestling mat, all I can do is concentrate on the person I'm up against. It's like my brain is just quiet for a little while. It's pretty cool." He puffs out his chest a little. "So I guess I'm a jock now."

I laugh so hard I wheeze. "Well, count me as your number one fan because . . . we are family," I belt at the top of my lungs.

He turns to me and holds the paper up as a fake microphone. "Get up everybody and sing!"

"Shut up!" Jorge shouts from the window upstairs.

CHAPTER THIRTY-FIVE

Dear Sweet Pea

I walk my bike home, and even though it's too hot to see straight, I feel excited for the first time in a long time about what the future holds, because I know that I've got Oscar by my side. And Kiera, too.

I walk past Dad's house and find that his work truck is gone, but Mr. Salcedo, his landlord, has parked his maroon Bronco alongside another car in the driveway.

The front door swings open and Greg walks out with his parents and Mr. Salcedo a few steps behind.

"Greg," I call out to him. "What are you doing here?"

He jogs down the walkway to me. "Hey, Sweet Pea! I forgot you live on this street. My parents are thinking about buying this place from Mr. Salcedo. They were waiting to get something more permanent until after we saw how my dad's new job panned out."

I look past him to his parents, who are older than any other parents from our class.

"So you might be my neighbor?" I ask. "Well, sort of my neighbor. I'm just one house down."

"Looks like it," he says with a grin.

The thought of Greg sleeping in the same room that used to be my second bedroom sets my cheeks aflame. "Cool." My voice squeaks.

He nods. "Very cool."

"I'll see you around, then?" I ask.

"Definitely. And there's seventh-grade graduation tomorrow night too."

"Oh yeah. You're right. I'll see you then." And I'm not even dreading it, because Mom actually found the dress I liked at Levine's online and in my size.

I walk past Miss Flora Mae's and give her two big thumbs up, and she gives me a devilish grin in return. We officially start on *Sweet Pea's Corner* next week. Miss Flora Mae even said I'll get paid! Not much, but more than my weekly allowance.

Before I go inside to collapse on the couch in the dark, cool living room, I check the mail.

One envelope sits inside. The outside is blank. No stamp or anything. Just an envelope that someone must have put in my mailbox themselves. I rest my bike against the fence and neatly tear open the envelope.

Dear Sweet Pea, the letter reads. I could use your advice . . .

Dear Reader,

Unlike Sweet Pea's letters, what I'm writing today is not about a dilemma waiting to be solved. Instead, I am overflowing with gratitude for all the people who helped make my piles of words into a book. If you can spare me just one more letter, I'd like to take a minute to say thank you.

Thank you to my editor, Alessandra Balzer, who guided me and cheered me on as I ventured out into the unknown world of middle grade. Thank you for being Cheese's biggest and most loyal fan.

John Cusick, thank you for your friendship and agenting prowess. A huge shout-out to everyone at Folio for all you do to keep the engines running behind the scenes!

I'm proud to call HarperCollins home, and the best part about Harper will always be the people. I owe so many of you endless gratitude for your faith in me and tireless work on my behalf. Thank you to Suzanne Murphy, Donna Bray, Andrea Pappenheimer, Kerry Moynagh, Kathy Faber, Patty Rosati, Ann Dye, Nellie Kurtzman, Robby Imfeld, Stephanie Macy, Lindsay Karl, Cindy Hamilton, Sari Murray, Liz Byer, Alison Donalty, Jenna Stempel-Lobell, Caitlin Johnson, Caitlin Garing, the HCC team, and the Harper360 team.

Thank you to Dana Spector, my favorite Hollywood insider and fellow INTJ!

I'd be a whole lump of nothing without the folks who

read this book early on and offered their invaluable feedback. Thank you to Dhonielle Clayton, Bethany Hagen, Mark Oshiro, and Natalie C. Parker. I'm so proud to count you as peers and friends.

In addition to my early readers, I'm lucky to have so many friends who are quick to offer a listening ear and much encouragement. I would like to especially thank Kristin Treviño, Tessa Gratton, Molly Cusick, Justina Ireland, Zoraida Cordova, Luke and Lauren Brewer (and all of Union Worx!), Corey Whaley, John Stickney, Ashley Meredith, Kristin Hahn, Veronica Treviño, Paul Samples, Emma Treviño, and Ashley Lindemann.

Thank you to my family, especially Mom for sharing your sense of adventure and Dad for your love of pizza and politics. I can't help but thank my furbabies, Dexter, Opie, and Rufus, for offering indiscriminate and endless cuddles. Like Sweet Pea, I have found much comfort in my furry companions.

And how could I forget my favorite person of all? Ian Pearce, thank you for being my partner in everything.

If, like the people whose letters Sweet Pea answered, you ever find yourself feeling a little stuck, I hope you always know that help is never far away. Whether it's a parent, a teacher, a librarian, a relative, or a friend, never be scared to ask for a little help.

Love,
One Incredibly Lucky Author (aka Julie)